"You're A Little Skittish This Morning, Doctor."

"And you're a little sneaky, Your Highness," Fran told him.

Max shot her a sideways glance. "Just a little?"

"Well, I was trying to be gracious. You know, you being the sovereign around here and all."

"Technically, I'm not the sovereign. That would be my father. But I understand your point." He stood and walked over to her, amusement glistening in his eyes. "Afraid I might lock you up i̶n̶ ̶t̶h̶e̶ ̶d̶u̶n̶g̶e̶o̶n̶?"

Fran tipped her ch̶i̶n̶.̶ ̶"̶I̶'̶m̶ ̶n̶o̶t̶ ̶a̶f̶r̶a̶i̶d̶ ̶o̶f̶ ̶a̶nything, Your Highnes̶s̶.̶ ̶I̶'̶m̶ ̶j̶u̶s̶t̶ ̶t̶r̶y̶i̶n̶g̶ ̶t̶o̶ ̶b̶e̶ ̶p̶o̶l̶i̶t̶e̶—"

"Who said any̶t̶h̶i̶n̶g̶ ̶a̶b̶o̶u̶t̶ ̶a̶ ̶d̶u̶n̶g̶e̶o̶n̶?̶"̶ ̶H̶e̶r̶ ̶e̶y̶e̶s̶ ̶w̶e̶n̶t̶ wide.

Awareness move̶d̶ ̶t̶h̶r̶o̶u̶g̶h̶ ̶h̶e̶r̶ like warm molasses. Why, oh why, did she have to turn to mush when this man was near? It just wasn't fair. She could control every aspect of her life, every emotion—every need. But here in Fantasyland with Prince Foxy, she was reduced to...well, female.

Dear Reader,

Revel in the month with a special day devoted to
L-O-V-E by enjoying six passionate, powerful and
provocative romances from Silhouette Desire.

Learn the secret of the Barone family's Valentine's Day
curse, in *Sleeping Beauty's Billionaire* (#1489) by
Caroline Cross, the second of twelve titles in the continuity
series DYNASTIES: THE BARONES—the saga of an elite
clan, caught in a web of danger, deceit…and desire.

In *Kiss Me, Cowboy!* (#1490) by Maureen Child, a delicious
baker feeds the desire of a marriage-wary rancher. And
passion flares when a detective and a socialite undertake a
cross–country quest, in *That Blackhawk Bride* (#1491), the
most recent installment of Barbara McCauley's popular
SECRETS! miniseries.

A no-nonsense vet captures the attention of a royal bent
on seduction, in *Charming the Prince* (#1492), the newest
"fiery tale" by Laura Wright. In Meagan McKinney's latest
MATCHED IN MONTANA title, *Plain Jane & the Hotshot*
(#1493), a shy music teacher and a daredevil fireman
make perfect harmony. And a California businessman finds
himself longing for his girl Friday every day of the week, in
At the Tycoon's Command (#1494) by Shawna Delacorte.

Celebrate Valentine's Day by reading all six of the steamy
new love stories from Silhouette Desire this month.

Enjoy!

Joan Marlow Golan

Joan Marlow Golan
Senior Editor, Silhouette Desire

Please address questions and book requests to:
Silhouette Reader Service
U.S.: 3010 Walden Ave., P.O. Box 1325, Buffalo, NY 14269
Canadian: P.O. Box 609, Fort Erie, Ont. L2A 5X3

Charming
the Prince
LAURA WRIGHT

Silhouette®

Desire.

Published by Silhouette Books

America's Publisher of Contemporary Romance

SILHOUETTE BOOKS

ISBN 0-373-76492-8

CHARMING THE PRINCE

Copyright © 2003 by Laura Wright

This edition published by arrangement with Harlequin Books S.A.

® and TM are trademarks of Harlequin Books S.A., used under license.
Trademarks indicated with ® are registered in the United States Patent
and Trademark Office, the Canadian Trade Marks Office and in other
countries.

Visit Silhouette at www.eHarlequin.com

Printed in U.S.A.

Books by Laura Wright

Silhouette Desire

Cinderella & the Playboy #1451
Hearts Are Wild #1469
Baby & the Beast #1482
Charming the Prince #1492

LAURA WRIGHT

has spent most of her life immersed in the world of acting, singing and competitive ballroom dancing. But when she started writing romance, she knew she'd found the true desire of her heart! Although born and raised in Minneapolis, Laura has also lived in New York City, Milwaukee and Columbus, Ohio. Currently, she is happy to have set down her bags and made Los Angeles her home. And a blissful home it is—one that she shares with her theater production manager husband, Daniel, and three spoiled dogs. During those few hours of downtime from her beloved writing, Laura enjoys going to art galleries and movies, cooking for her hubby, walking in the woods, lazing around lakes, puttering in the kitchen and frolicking with her animals. Laura would love to hear from you. You can write to her at P.O. Box 5811 Sherman Oaks, CA 91413 or e-mail her at laurawright@laurawright.com.

To my own Prince Charming, Daniel.
You make life a fairy tale for me every day.
To my new friends, and wonderful authors,
Kristi Gold and Bronwyn Jameson. You guys are the
best. And to Lois J. Thomasson of Fleetwind
Wolfhounds. Thank you for helping me to understand the
glorious wolfhound. I'm still waiting for my puppy!

One

Francesca Charming didn't believe in fairy tales, despite her whimsical surname. But with real-life royal cobblestones under her feet, the purple-and-gold Llandaron flag snapping crisply in the warm morning wind and the ancient fortress standing regally before her, a girl could change her mind.

The seven-story castle of white stone and polished elegance sat high on a bluff overlooking the Atlantic coastline. Rows of creamy-marble steps crept up, up, until they reached a massive wooden portcullis. Hundreds of windows peeked out at Fran through their frames of slender evergreen climbers, while on both ends of the amazing dwelling, two white towers extended their pepper-pot necks toward an azure sky.

And all around her, the scents of heather and saltwater carried on the breeze slowly lulling her from all thoughts of business, of why she'd come to—

"Welcome to Llandaron, miss."

Fran jumped at the spirited burr, whirled around. A gardener pruning a wedge of fragrant honeysuckle gave her a wink. "First time to the castle, eh? Surely takes the breath away, doesn't it?"

The magic from a moment ago vanished and reality set in. Indulging in a child's fantasy was not why Fran had come to Llandaron. She'd come to the small island nation to work—to earn the money that would finally put the wheels of a lifelong dream in motion. And Fran's dream, her one and only goal, was to open a Los Angeles-based animal-surgery facility.

Gripping her veterinary bag tightly to her side, she smiled at the gardener and said in her most professional tone, "Yes, I'm Dr. Charming. I just arrived this morning. I'm looking for the stables. Am I going the right way?"

The gardener clipped her a nod. "Just keep following the path you're on and you'll run straight into it. Make sure to ask for Charlie when you get down there. He runs things." The man turned away to tend to a young fir tree. "He'll show you round."

"Thank you." Fran turned and continued down the stone path, her traitorous gaze once again lapping up every detail she encountered.

All the books she'd read on Llandaron boasted of its "lush, wild beauty in the spring." But such a description didn't do the land justice. As she walked through a manicured garden that sloped gently toward the grand-looking stables, she took in the impossibly green lawns in the distance, small curves of hill blooming scads of tiny red flowers, and chunks of purple heather that dwelled amongst groomed shrubbery and ancient trees.

Only a hundred miles from Cornwall, England, Llandaron seemed a world away.

Gripping her black bag more tightly, Fran walked into the streamlined stables with what she hoped was an air of confidence. Horses nickered at her from their exceptionally clean stalls, and she allowed herself the time to give each a soft rub on their blazes before she marched down a lengthy hallway looking for a man called Charlie.

But when she came to the last stall, she stopped dead in her tracks. As she stared at the amazing sight before her, her knees went butter soft, and her throat desert dry as her pulse kicked and punched in her veins.

Pitchfork in hand, his bare back to her, a man was scooping up hay and tossing the tawny flakes into an adjacent stall. With no thought of what she was doing, Fran let her gaze travel from scuffed boots upward to faded jeans that encased strong, muscular thighs and, Lord almighty, one fine, fine backside. She licked her lips, her gaze progressing. He had a tapered waist and a broad, tanned back that bunched with lean muscle and glistened with sweat.

She released a soft sigh of appreciation. To her dismay, the man turned at the sound, saw her staring and grinned.

"Hello there." The brogue was native Llandaron,

the words slipping from his firm, sensual lips like melted chocolate, coating her senses in a very satisfying heat.

Fran struggled to find her voice. Tongue-tied and awestruck was not her usual style around men. Aloof and impassive was what she strove for, but this six-foot god, with his thick, wavy black hair, chiseled features and thick brows positioned over deep-set Prussian-blue eyes, wasn't like any man she'd ever seen.

Her gaze dipped to his chest, dusted with hair and thickly muscled. He had what the girls in her office called a six-pack. Truly sigh worthy, she mused as she balled her hands into fists to keep them from reaching out to feel that chest, feel those muscles bunch and flex beneath her palms.

With every ounce of fortitude she possessed, she cleared her throat and adopted a confident tone. "You must be Charlie."

He leaned casually against the door frame, his steady gaze warming her blood. "I must?"

From his tone, Fran couldn't tell if his reply was a question or an answer, but she didn't press the matter. There was no way she was going to let this guy know how flustered and unsure he made her feel. "I'm Dr. Francesca Charming—Fran, actually."

Comprehension lit those magnetic eyes of his. "The veterinarian from America."

"California."

His wicked blue gaze traveled lazily over her until he paused at her mouth. "Blond hair, tanned skin, long legs and beautiful eyes. A California girl."

Her unsophisticated beige pants and blue wrinkle-free blouse suddenly felt like black, lacy, racy lingerie. She felt a blush creep into her cheeks and she willed it away. For Pete's sake, she was a city girl. She didn't blush or twitter like a blue jay in the spring. She gave guys with too much cockiness a good dressing-down—of course, all the while hoping they couldn't tell that one big wimp resided behind her self-possessed facade.

"Have you had enough of a look?" she asked, tipping her chin up a fraction. "Or would you like me to turn around?"

His gaze lifted to meet hers, his expression littered with amusement. "I think I should be asking you the same thing."

She swallowed thickly. True enough.

A smile tugged at his lips. "Well?"

"Well, what?"

He drew a circle in the air with one long tapered finger. "You did make the offer, Dr. Charming. And I think it's only fair you show me yours after you had such a long look at mine."

Her eyes went wide. "I did no such thing! And…well, there is no way I'm going to turn…I was just…that wasn't meant as a—"

He grinned. "Maybe some other time, then."

"I don't think so."

She looked away, searching for the reason she'd come to Llandaron. Her gaze scanned the large office to her right with its comfortable furnishing and windows on every wall, then paused as she finally saw what she was looking for. Over by an open bay window, lying on six feet of plush green whelping bed was a pretty wolfhound with a fat belly and liquid-brown eyes. A patch of sun filtered into the room through the window screen, bathing the dog in pale light.

Ten days ago Fran had never heard of King Oliver or his wolfhound—goodness, she'd barely heard of Llandaron—until her partner and could-be-fiancé, Dr. Dennis Cavanaugh, was offered the "royal" post. Dennis's reputation with the pets of the rich and famous in Los Angeles had earned him invitations to fancy places all the time. But this particular time, he was too occupied with a certain young film star's bichon frise to leave the country. So he'd recommended Fran for the job. With the generous fee and her need for a little breathing room, she hadn't had to think too long or too hard about the offer.

The wolfhound glanced up at Fran then, perhaps wondering who she was and why she'd come. Fran smiled. "Well, aren't you a beauty," she said, walking the few steps to the office doorway and reaching for the handle on the gate that separated them.

But before she could lift the latch, a large hand clamped over hers, sending a jolt of heat spiraling up her arm. "Allow me, Doctor."

A soft gasp escaped Fran's throat as she snatched her hand out from under his.

"I hope I didn't burn you," he said with dry humor, opening the gate and allowing her entrance.

She walked swiftly past him. "You did nothing."

The man chuckled and muttered a husky, "Are you sure?"

Fran walked over to her patient, her cheeks flaming. Embarrassment swam in her blood—at her silly reaction to his touch and at the out-and-out lie that his simple hand-over-hand contact did nothing to her.

If she had her druthers, she'd tell him right here, right now that he could take off, that she could handle things from here. But she knew that the wolfhound would be far more at ease with someone she knew, and the dog's health was more important than some annoying and unwelcome palpitations.

"So you're my patient?" Fran said with practiced calm, sitting down beside the very pregnant wolfhound. The unease she felt in the company of the stimulating stable hand began to evaporate. She was with her patient—she was where she belonged.

"Her name is Grand Dame Glindaron." In seconds the man was at her side, bending down, his faded jeans pulling taut against his muscular thighs, his previously naked chest now covered with a worn black T-shirt. "But we call her Glinda."

"Glinda, huh?" Fran reached out and let the dog sniff her hand. "As in the good witch?"

"The good witch?" the man repeated.

"You know, *The Wizard of Oz.*" She glanced over at him. "Glinda the good witch?" None of this seemed to be registering. "It's a movie."

He sat back on his heels. "Ah, we don't get those here."

Her eyes went wide. "What?"

He gave her a sinful grin.

"Very funny, Charlie," she said dryly.

He looked down at the floor for a moment, and

Fran felt relieved—like finding a patch of shade from the blistering sun—yet she couldn't drag her gaze away from him. That highly kissable mouth, killer body. Such a package was lethal for a woman who had sworn off sex appeal in favor of sweet-natured.

With all her might, Fran tried to conjure up an image of Dennis. But it was no use. The stable hand's mesmerizing eyes were powerful and persistent. If the guy ever wanted to quit working at the stables and go into hypnosis, he could probably make a fortune.

"Actually, Llandaroners love a good movie," the man was saying as he gave Glinda a good scratch behind her ear. "The royal family, as well. And in fact, *The Wizard of Oz* is purported to be the king's favorite."

"I'm glad to know that His Majesty has good taste. In movies *and* in animals." Opening her medical bag, Fran took out a thermometer and a stethoscope. She'd given Glinda a few moments to relax, get accustomed to her voice and movement. It was time to get to work, and if the disturbing stable hand was going to hang around, she'd just have to grin and bear it.

After today, she and Glinda would be at ease with each other, and Fran wouldn't have to see or talk to the guy again.

"Do you take care of Glinda?" she asked, switching into doctor mode.

"I keep a close eye on her."

"Then I'd like to ask you a few questions, if I may."

He inclined his head. "Of course."

"Is she eating and drinking?"

"Eating less, drinking more."

Fran nodded. "Has she had any bleeding, vomiting or diarrhea?"

"No."

"All right." She scooted closer to the hound. "Why don't you pet her, keep her calm, while I take a listen and a look."

He raised an amused brow. "Are you asking me to assist you, Doctor?"

"If you don't mind."

"Why would I mind?"

"I certainly don't want to take you away from your work," she explained.

"My work?"

She gestured toward the stables. "Cleaning the stalls and feeding the animals…"

"Ah, yes, of course. My work." His eyes glinted blue fire. "I think I can spare a few minutes."

Awareness stirred in her belly, deep and low—in a place so foreign she was caught off guard for a moment. But she fought her way back. "All right, but I don't want to get you into any trouble with your boss, so let me know if I'm taking up too much of your time."

"That's very considerate," he said on a dry chuckle. "But there's nothing to worry about. My employer and I are on very good terms."

After taking the wolfhound's temperature, Fran listened to her heart and lungs and the sound of the sweet little pups in her belly. She took her time with the incredibly healthy wolfhound, thankful to have a break from the sexy stable hand for a moment. Never in her life had she been so affected or so attracted. Surely not with any of the good-looking men in L.A. Not even with Dennis.

"Wolfhounds can have fairly high-risk pregnancies," the man said when Fran took off her stethoscope and began checking the wolfhound's eyes and ears. "I understand that you're a specialist in such cases."

"That rumor is true."

"There are others?" He leaned closer to Glinda as Fran opened the dog's mouth to check her teeth.

"Sure." She played along, keeping the mood light, while she tried desperately not to take in the man's delectable scent. Suede and virile male. "But they're all lies or at the very least, half-truths."

"I still wouldn't mind hearing them."

She pressed her lips together thoughtfully. "I don't think they'd be appropriate subject matter for the sweet and innocent subjects of Llandaron."

The heavy-lidded look he shot her way clearly stated that he was neither sweet nor innocent.

As if she didn't know that.

"What do you think of Llandaron, Dr. Charming?" he asked, his face a mere whisper from hers.

"Well, I've only been here for a few hours, but what I have seen is..." Suddenly her breath caught as his gaze dropped brazenly to her mouth.

"Impressive?" he asked, his gruff baritone wrapping around her like silk on steel.

"Yes," she answered in some kind of hazy whisper that she'd heard women use in the movies, but had never heard come out of her own mouth.

What was happening here? she thought wildly as a sudden flash of salty air rushed through the open window. What the devil was happening to her? Maybe she should've stayed in Los Angeles with Dennis, let someone else take the job.

Fran thrust that irrational thought away. So she was attracted to this man. It happened. It didn't mean she was going to do anything about it or, more importantly, let it interfere with her job.

"Llandaron is rather impressive," the man said, nudging her out of her self-analysis. "The people are proud of their country. Its unmarred beauty and peaceful existence."

"They should be proud. It's an amazing place." She returned to Glinda, stroking the wolfhound's wiry gray fur, eager for the dog to get comfortable with her. "Have you lived here all your life?"

"In Llandaron or here in the palace?"

"Either one."

"Yes to both."

"So you grew up in style, huh?" she said on a soft chuckle. "Your parents worked here and now you do?"

"Some would call it the family business."

She couldn't help herself. She glanced over at him, her brow furrowed. "That sounded almost regretful."

"One's choices in life are not always his own, Doctor."

"That is such bunk," she shot back.

He chuckled. "You think so?"

"Yes, I do." Glinda put her head on Fran's knee and closed her eyes. "We have one chance at this life. Giving others control over it—control over something as precious as our choices—is a waste."

"Of time?"

"Of life." Once she started on a subject like this, she couldn't be stopped. "My father always said, 'Life's a gift.'" Fran's heart squeezed painfully at the thought of her father. He'd been gone almost sixteen years, died and left her alone with a non-family who barely remembered her name. But even so, her love for him remained resolute.

The man beside her watched her intently, his expression shuttered. "What about the king's children, Doctor? To them, duty and honor must come first. They don't have the luxury of choice."

"Of course they do. They just chose the duty and honor over their wants and needs." Just as she had chosen sweet and steady Dennis over the smooth talkers who only wanted one thing, then moved on to their next conquest after they got it. No fairy tales or fairy-tale princes for her. Just lots of wolves in Armani clothing. Thank God, she'd only fallen for their silver-tongued appeal once.

She returned her attention to Glinda, feeling her belly, and the little puppies that grew there. "It's funny, most people romanticize the royals—the lifestyle—the parties and balls, the perfect kisses and the handsome prince and all that."

"But not you?"

"No." She stayed in safe territory with her response. "When I was young, I didn't sit in front of a Disney cartoon enraptured like other little girls did."

"What did you do, instead?"

Fran couldn't help but smile. "Made splints for the injured animals that found their way into our yard."

"And I'll bet you cured every one." Gentle humor laced his tone.

"Most. But some things were beyond my control." Like her stepbrothers' cruel games and tricks, hiding her precious animals until she cried and begged for their return.

Fran forced the past back where it belonged and adopted a relaxed smile. "Let's just say that I've never been one to see things through a rosy glow."

"How do you see things, Francesca?"

"It's just Fran," she told him again. "And I see life through a pair of infrared sunglasses. I want to see the details, the truth. I don't want to be blinded by fantasy."

"You know, fantasies can be very fulfilling."

Heat coiled low in her belly at his words. Without thinking, she looked up into his dark-blue eyes, eyes that held passion and intelligence. "In the short term, perhaps."

A grin touched his lips. "And you don't look for short-term pleasures?"

Her gaze flickered to the window, then down at Glinda, anywhere but on him. "Are we still talking about my views on life?"

"How old are you, Francesca?"

"Twenty-eight."

"You know, you're very wise for such a young woman."

She shrugged, slightly embarrassed by his compliment. "I just know my own mind, that's all."

"Very progressive."

"Is it?"

His smile went wide. "Yes, I think so."

"Pardon me, Your Highness."

Fran's gaze shot to the doorway, where an older man dressed in work clothes stood, a green tam atop his graying hair, his eyes large and curious.

"Good morning, Charlie," came the baritone beside her, his tone now laden with formality.

Fran's heart dropped like a stone.

Charlie bowed low. "Good morning, Your Highness. His Royal Highness has returned from town and wishes to speak with you."

"Thank you, Charlie. You may go."

Fran didn't wait for the real Charlie to leave. She whirled around, faced the man who she'd assumed was the stable hand, the man she'd sat here staring at, drooling over, chatting with and advising on the important things in life.

She narrowed her eyes at him. "Your Highness?"

"I didn't get a chance to properly introduce myself." He inclined his head, but those devilish blue eyes remained locked on hers. "Prince Maxim Stephan Henry Thorne."

Two

Maxim watched the American beauty's eyes turn a deep brown, and once again he cursed the bargain he'd made with his father almost a year ago. Why the hell would he ever get married to some humorless blue blood of the court when there were women such as this around to tempt him?

Never in his life had he met a woman as full of acuity and opinions as this one. Normally he didn't find those characteristics appealing, but with her…

He let his gaze move over her. She sat there, clearly annoyed by what he'd just told her—or not told her—a band of sunlight illuminating her amazing features. Shimmering blond waves caressed those stubborn shoulders, while a heart-shaped face sported high cheekbones and satin skin. She was slim, but ripe in all the right places. And when she'd walked past him into the office a few minutes ago, an arrow of blood-pumping desire had struck him dead center—not to mention a few inches lower.

But there was one feature she possessed that made him want to howl at the moon: her mouth, that pink upside-down fantasy with its lush upper lip.

"Your Highness?"

Her irritated query jolted him from his reverie. "Yes, Doctor?"

"You tricked me."

He nodded. "Yes."

"I don't like being tricked," she said sternly. "I had enough of it growing up." A quick blush crept to her cheeks, but she continued. "I'm not about to take any more of it now. From a prince *or* a stable boy."

Maxim stared at her, thoroughly amused. He'd never been spoken to in such a way. Women didn't scold him. They flirted and complimented and went to bed with him. "I apologize."

She hesitated for a moment, and he wondered if she was going to toss his apology back in his face. But she didn't. Instead, a look of confusion sprang to her eyes. "You were pitching hay."

He shrugged. "I like the distraction."

"From what? This perfect place you live in?"

"No place is perfect, Doctor."

She expelled a weighty breath, a yielding breath. "So, what am I supposed to do now?"

"I'm not sure I understand the question."

"If you think I'm going to stand up and curtsy after what you just pulled—"

"I wouldn't hear of it." He grinned, standing himself. "Not now, anyway."

"Try not ever!" She jerked to her feet without waiting for him to offer a hand. Though Maxim sincerely doubted if she would've actually taken his help had he had the time to offer it.

"Perhaps around the court or my father you could at least...nod?"

She paused, then said, "We'll see."

His grin widened. "Thank you."

They stood facing each other, Glinda's watchful gaze on them. Francesca was tall, maybe three inches shorter than him. A perfect height for a man to lean in and—

"I have to know," she said, folding her arms across her splendid chest. "Why didn't you tell me who you are? Was playing me like that just another distraction?"

She stood close, so close he could feel the heat of her body, breathe in that soft almost honeylike scent of her. "Truthfully, I wanted to know what it was like to be anonymous."

"And how was it?"

"Invigorating."

"Well, I'm glad I could help," she said wryly.

"You're sure you're not going to treat me differently now that you know the truth?"

"My conscience and my pride would suffer a great indignity if I treated you as anything more than the prankster you've shown yourself to be."

"And we wouldn't want that." Grinning, Maxim walked over to the desk in the far corner and seized the paperwork he'd been working on before he'd gotten frustrated and taken a break in the stalls. When he turned back to face Francesca, he said, "It was nice to meet you, Doctor. I'm sure we'll be seeing each other again."

She fairly chuckled. "And who will you be next time?"

He raised a brow. "I've always had a longing to try my hand at masonry."

"Sounds perfect."

"On second thought," he said, his mouth carving into a smile. "Sounds a little too far away from the stables for my liking." He inclined his head, then turned to leave.

She called back, "Not at all, Your Highness."

Maxim paused, glanced over his shoulder. "Such a lofty title doesn't seem right after the informal tête-à-tête we've just shared."

"Prince Maxim, then?" she offered, baiting him.

"How about just Maxim?"

She grinned. "How about just Max?"

"I don't think so." That smile of hers gripped him tightly and held, while her mouth stirred his blood. He knew he'd better leave while he still could. "Goodbye, Francesca."

She dropped into a funny-looking curtsy. "Goodbye, Max."

For the first time in a long time, Maxim laughed, deeply and genuinely. And he kept it up long after he'd left the room, walked down the hallway and stepped out into the kingdom he called home.

*   *   *

Fran stood in front of the full-length mirror in her opulent blue bedroom in the east wing of the castle and rolled her eyes at her reflection.

The chagrin she felt had nothing whatever to do with the eye-catching chocolate-brown dress and matching boots she wore or the sassy swept-up hair-style that one of her vet techs had repeatedly told her looked "hot." Nope, the roll of the eyes was for the hope she felt. The hope of seeing a certain prince again.

Oh, Lord. A prince.

Was she crazy? Had the untainted Llandaron air turned her normally sensible and analytical brain to mush? Even if she could forget for a moment that Max was royalty and lived on Fantasy Island, why wasn't she thinking about Dennis? Sure, there was no actual commitment between them yet. But before she'd left, he'd asked her to marry him—and she'd said she'd think about it. True, they weren't exactly in love, but that was because neither one of them believed in the concept. Dennis had also been burned—by the female equivalent to Fran's smooth talker.

Consequently, she and Dennis were no longer romantics.

They were scientists.

Shoot, their common viewpoints and careers were why they had become such good friends in the first place. This way they would be two *great* friends forming an everlasting bond, caring for and support-ing one another.

And then she'd had to come here and run into a real live Prince Charming!

An image of Max splintered through her mind. Those eyes, that touch, those lips…

Was he married? The random thought was followed by a shiver, and she turned away from the mirror. The marital status of His Highness was none of her business; nothing about him was her business. Glinda and the pups were her business. And heck, she probably wouldn't see him again, anyway. He had…royal stuff to do with other royals. He didn't have time to hang around the stables every day with some commoner from California.

Speaking of time, Fran checked her watch. Five minutes to six.

She'd met with the king more than an hour ago. A feisty old bear with intelligent blue eyes just like his son's. After receiving a full report on Glinda's stellar health, he'd told Fran that she was to have dinner with him at six o'clock and not to be late.

Good Lord, she thought as she left her room and darted down the long staircase, she'd had no idea that she would be eating with the king of Llandaron. She'd figured it would be dinner on a tray in her room every night. Or in the kitchen with the rest of the employees.

Below her, a shadow came into the grand hallway, large and imposing. Her pulse bumped and skittered as the heel of her boot touched down on the last stair step.

"Good evening, Francesca."

Ignoring the warmth pinging urgently in her stomach, she started with, "Good evening, M…" But the greeting died on her lips as her gaze took in the proverbial handsome prince who stood regally in the center of the marble hall.

She gripped the edge of the banister for a little extra support. Handsome didn't even begin to cover it. Her fingers itched to run wild through his thick black hair, her gaze longed to search the depths of deep-set blue eyes. Gone were the jeans and T-shirt he'd worn today. In their place breathed a crisp white dress shirt, black jacket and pants with a break so fine it would make a London tailor sigh.

But there was no tailor in sight, so Fran sighed, instead, her mind racing ahead with thoughts like, Now, *this* is what I'd like for dinner.

"You look beautiful tonight, Doctor," Max said, his eyes roaming the length of her. "Care for an escort?"

For a moment, she saw herself standing beside him, slipping her hand through his arm, feeling the muscles in his biceps flex against her fingers. But the moment passed. "Thanks, but I can manage."

He raised a dark brow. "Is it just me, or do you have a problem with all men who show you an ounce of chivalry?"

"No, it's just you." The retort came out fast and unplanned, and she wondered if she'd offended him.

But Max only grinned at her impudence. "Come with me," he said, starting for the door, which was being held open by a stoic older gentleman in black tie and tails.

Fran glanced first at the open door, then at Max. "Come with you where?"

"Out."

"But the king invited me—"

"My father is on the phone with the president of Lithuania. He sends his regrets and has asked me to entertain you."

"Oh, he did, did he?" The remark was calm, but beneath her cool exterior, her heart pounded fiercely. Entertain her how?

"Stop being so suspicious," he said, a grin pulling at his full lips. "I promised you no more tricks."

"All right," she said, walking toward him. "I *am* pretty hungry."

He chuckled. "And I'm flattered."

"Where are we going?" Into town maybe? She'd read about several wonderful restaurants and ice-cream shops, and even a taffy shop. But did royalty go to town for a meal?

"We're going to the lighthouse," he said as he ushered her past and out the door.

Sounded like a restaurant. Nice seafood place with... Fran paused, her surroundings seizing her attention. Milky-white clouds had taken over the sky and sunset, riding low and thick on the ground.

"What happened here?" Fran asked on a laugh, standing dead center in the haze.

"Fog."

"Fog? But the sun was so bright today, no clouds at all. When did this come on?" She turned around once, feeling the cool mist against her skin. "It's as dense as cotton candy. I can hardly see five feet in front of me.''

Max took her hand in his. ''You'll get used to it.''

''I will?'' she asked lamely, her mind and every one of her senses focused on the feel of Max's large warm hand. Maybe she should've pulled free, sent a message to him and to herself that touching of any kind was inappropriate. But she didn't. She forgot about a jacket, a purse, all things practical and held on, just let him guide her across the lawn and away from the castle.

''When my ancestors first came to this land,'' he began, ''the elders of both the Thorne and Brunell royal families wanted their firstborn children to marry. But the Thornes' eldest daughter, Sana, was deeply in love with another man, a poor ship worker, and her father strictly forbade her to see him again. On the day before her wedding, Sana took her life.'' Max's hand tightened around Fran's. ''That night was the first time the fog came.''

''Is that a legend?'' Fran asked, awe threading her query.

''No. A fact. History.'' Max guided her around a large rock. ''From then to now, the fog rolls in at six every night and disappears by seven. Many have said that the one hour of cover is granted by Sana for all ill-fated lovers. For that one hour, they can meet without fear of being discovered.''

Wonder moved through Fran, taking hold of the soft parts of her heart, and she couldn't stop herself from asking, ''Have you ever met anyone in the fog?''

He chuckled and said, "Not until today," as he led her expertly through the grounded cloudbank.

And just as she realized that they weren't going to town, the scent of the ocean hit her. She stopped and faced Max. "I thought you said no more tricks."

His gaze impaled her. "This is no trick, Francesca."

"Then what are we doing here?"

"I live here."

He led her forward a few paces until she saw it.

Barely visible through the fog were the first two stories of a lighthouse. A lighthouse that she imagined was tall and imposing—just like its owner. Warm, inviting light spilled through the windows, beckoning them to come inside.

Without a word, Max guided her up a set of stone stairs, across a bed of rocks, then through a massive oak door and into the lighthouse.

"You live here?" she asked, wonder thick in her voice. "And not in the palace?"

"I prefer to live alone," he said, releasing her hand.

Being free of his grasp was a strange sensation. In one respect she was relieved to have the heat, the strength, gone. But in another respect, she felt displaced, as if a part of her remained with him when he'd dropped her hand.

Fran followed him up the lovely spiral staircase to what she guessed to be the second floor of a three-story dwelling. Persian rugs covered polished hardwood floors, and comfortable couches in deep shades of plum sat facing each other, a rich mahogany chest between them. A marble fireplace took up most of one wall, and a cluster of windows the size of computer screens another. While still another wall boasted French doors, which hung open, allowing the cool ocean breeze to filter into the room, only mildly upsetting the gold cloth napkins which rested atop what appeared to be solid gold plates on a small mahogany dining table. A table set elegantly for two.

"This is magnificent," Fran said. "You've done a wonderful job with this space."

"Thank you. It was a labor of love. I always coveted the lighthouse when I was a child, escaped here when I had the chance. And when Llandaron no longer had use for it, I converted it into my home." He walked over to the table and held out a chair for her. "May I?" He grinned devilishly. "I promise I won't pull it out the minute you sit down."

She couldn't help the smile that came to her lips. "I appreciate that." This whole scenario was surreal—the beautifully set table in front of the prime ocean view—and Fran had to warn herself as she sat down on the plush cushion of plum silk, that she'd better remember who she was and where she'd come from—and more importantly, that a real live prince sat across from her.

In seconds, a woman with a mop of graying hair and a pleasant smile appeared and placed several wonderful-smelling items in front of them.

After thanking the woman, Fran turned to Max and whispered, "Cheeseburgers, French fries and beer?"

He picked up a fry and winked. "An American meal for your first night away from home."

She laughed as she placed her napkin in her lap. Burgers and fries on a solid gold plate—too funny.

"I have soda if you would rather not drink alcohol," Max said.

"No, this is great."

Though Max dug right in, Fran didn't start eating right away. For just a moment, she watched the prince of Llandaron as he picked up his gourmet cheeseburger and went for it like any red-blooded American male. But in this case looks were incredibly deceiving. The guy with ketchup on his lip wasn't red-blooded at all, he was blue-blooded. And her attraction to him had to be controlled. She didn't trust this royal playboy as far as she could throw him, and she sure didn't trust her feelings and actions when she was around him.

"Anything wrong, Francesca?"

Her gaze snapped up. "Pardon me?"

"You're not eating, and you look as though you have something to say."

Something to say, something to say... She opted for small talk. "Have you ever been to America, Your Highness?"

"Many times. I own several companies there."

"You do?" she asked, surprised.

"I do work, Francesca." He chuckled. "Not at being a royal, but being a citizen of the world. My companies manufacture air- and water-purifying systems for office buildings and hotels. I've wanted to develop a way to keep the world and the people in it healthy ever since I could remember. Strange goal for a child, perhaps, but nothing deterred me." He tilted his head. "I imagine your need to care for animals started when you were very young, as well."

Fran took a sip of her beer and nodded. "When I first saw a baby squirrel with its leg caught in a trap, I was hooked. I had cages set up in my backyard." She nibbled on a French fry. "It's crazy, but after I helped that squirrel, more and more animals found their way into my yard."

"The word spread throughout the animal kingdom."

She nodded. "I truly believe they sought me out, that they knew I was committed to helping them."

"Of course they did." Max said the words with such conviction, Fran paused. Usually when she said something "out there," people laughed and thought she was kidding or, worse, a bit nuts. Dennis always made jokes about her claims that she could actually sense what an animal was feeling at times.

Max took a pull on his beer. "So you went to veterinary school, and then…"

"Then Dennis and I opened our own practice."

"Dennis?"

"My…well, he's a very good friend, a good man, really." She sounded like an imbecile. And why wasn't she telling him that Dennis was practically her fiancé? "Dennis is…well, he's practical and efficient, and he's great with animals."

"He sounds boring."

She shook her head. "He's not boring. He's…"

"I know," he said, grinning. "Practical and efficient."

She shot him a sidelong glance. "Men don't have

to be rich and handsome and royal to be attractive to a woman, Your Highness.''

Those killer blue eyes fairly lapped her up. ''You think I'm handsome?''

More than anything in the world she wanted to look away, but his gaze held hers. She wanted to grab her burger and stuff it into her reckless mouth, but her appetite was gone—her appetite for food, anyway. She needed to get away from him, away from this carnal, marvelous magic that surrounded him.

''What I think…is that I'm full.'' She stood up and dropped her napkin on the table. ''I'm really tired. It was a long flight, a long day, and I'm not looking to make this a long night, so…'' She stopped talking, realizing how she sounded.

Max grinned. ''I'll walk you back.''

''I think I can find the way.'' She looked out the window. Had to be after seven. ''The fog's cleared up.''

But the man was a prince, a gentleman, and he walked her back, anyway. Not to her bedroom door, thank goodness, because for the first time since the ''smooth talker,'' Fran felt what could be categorized as a surge of wildness. And she wasn't altogether sure if she could stop herself from grabbing Max by the shirtfront and pulling him inside.

''Are you going to marry her?''

Maxim had just said good-night to Francesca in the very same hall where their evening had begun. He was keyed-up, craving something he shouldn't even be contemplating, and in no mood for a go-round with his father. But he couldn't very well pass the man's door without speaking, so he stood in the library doorway. "Am I going to marry whom?"

"The duchess of Claymore."

"No." One night with the woman had been more than enough.

The king sighed and leaned back in his chair. "Do I have to remind you of our agreement?"

A muscle flicked in Maxim's jaw. "No."

"Eleven months ago we sat here in this very library and talked about the importance of having both my sons married. I gave you a year to find yourself a bride, and I distinctly recall you nodding your head." The king took off his reading glasses and regarded his son seriously. "You have one month left, Maxim. If you don't find a suitable woman to marry in that time, I swear I will choose for you."

"I have not met anyone I would even consider marrying, Father," he said with deadly calm. "I suggest we drop this before we both lose our tempers."

"I will not drop this. Your brother has been married for five years now and has yet to produce an heir. This is duty, Maxim, and you know it. What you owe to your country. If you love this land, you will do what needs to be done."

Pure unadulterated anger rippled through Maxim as he stared at the man who made him see red—the man he loved and respected above all others, the man who had had the good fortune to fall in love with the woman who was to be his queen. How could such a man expect his child to have anything less?

Five years ago, when his brother, Alex, had married, Maxim had thought that he would be free of honor and duty and marriage to a woman he cared nothing for. But when three years passed with no heir for Alex and his wife, Maxim knew what was in store for him. Llandaron was a small country, always in danger of getting sucked up by its larger and more powerful neighbors. Llandaron needed autonomy. Their citizens relied on a good and caring government. They relied on the stability of the royal family.

But dammit, he would not marry a woman he didn't love. And considering the fact that he'd never gotten close to such an emotion in all his thirty-five years, he didn't expect to find it anytime soon.

The king shook his head and sighed. "I don't understand you. There are hundreds of exquisite women in the kingdom to choose from."

The words of a pretty American veterinarian rang loudly in his ears. *We have one chance at this life. And giving others control over it is a waste.* She'd insisted people had choices. Maxim raked a hand through his hair. Regular folk had choices, but did a prince? Did a man who loved his country? Or did he sacrifice his personal needs for the needs of his country?

"Make no mistake about it, Maxim," the king said firmly. "Three weeks from Saturday, on the night of the masquerade ball, you will announce your bride-to-be. Or I will."

Maxim's jaw clenched tight. The man was relentless. Bride. And a suitable bride no less.

Suitable.

The word scratched at the door of his mind. Would his father back down if the woman was *un*suitable?

Maxim glanced up. "You will abide by my choice, Father?" he asked sharply.

The king nodded. "Of course."

Maxim nodded his good-night and left the room. Dr. Francesca Charming had intrigued, amused and attracted the hell out of him from the moment he'd first laid eyes on her. And the thought of seducing her brought a smile to his lips and a throbbing tension to the lower half of him.

It was the best of both worlds.

Having Francesca in his bed while putting the subject of marriage to rest with his father once and for all.

Three

Backlit by the warm, midmorning sunlight, Glinda gazed up at Fran, her brown eyes wide and needful.

"I won't let anything happen to you or your precious babies," Fran whispered, stroking the dog's wiry fur.

Instantly Glinda relaxed on her velvet mat, her eyes closing partway. Fran ached to lie down beside the sweet animal and maybe catch some of the shut-eye she'd missed last night.

Images of castles and princes, lighthouses and cartoon teapots singing about love, had filled her mind from midnight to dawn. Then, just as the sun had peeked its bald head up from the horizon, she'd fallen into a deep, dreamless sleep. It'd been close to eight when she'd awoken in her massive bed—to which the phrase king-size truly applied. Fran recalled how she'd smiled at that irony—a king-size bed in the Kingdom of Llandaron. At last she'd slipped out of that bed—literally—and hightailed it down to the stables.

Chuckling, Fran rose to her feet and filled Glinda's water bowl. Who slept in silk sheets and satin pillowcases, anyway? Not a woman who wore flannel pajamas with imprints of different animal paws all over them, that was for sure.

"How is your patient today, Doctor?"

Fran jumped, nearly spilling the water bowl. It was little wonder, with that husky burr of a baritone enveloping her like a magical and highly seductive cape.

Prince Maxim was lounging in the doorway, dressed in dark-blue jeans, white shirt and black blazer. His self-assured smile brought a girlish stain of pink to her cheeks.

"You seem a little skittish this morning, Doctor." He pushed away from the doorjamb, walked over to Glinda and gave her head a gentle pat.

Fran watched him bend down, watched his jeans pull snug on that fine, firm and very royal backside. "And you're a little sneaky, Your Highness."

He shot her a sideways glance. "Just a little?"

"Well, I was trying to be gracious. You know, you being the sovereign around here and all."

"Technically, I'm not the sovereign. That would be my father. But I take your point." He rose and walked over to her, amusement glittering in his eyes. "Afraid I might lock you up in a dungeon?"

She lifted her chin. "I'm not afraid of anything,

Your Highness. Even being locked up all alone in—''

''Who said anything about alone?'' He grinned broadly.

Awareness moved through her like warm molasses. Why, oh, why did she have to turn to mush when this man was near? It just wasn't fair. She could control every aspect of her life, every emotion, every need. But here in Fantasyland with Prince Foxy, she was reduced to…well, a mess of female hormones.

''So,'' he raised a brow, ''how about some lunch?''

Her gaze flickered to the wolfhound. ''I think I'm just going to share this yummy bowl of kibble with Glinda.''

He followed her gaze. ''That looks like one of Charlie's special blends.''

''It is. He brought it in just a few minutes ago.''

Max nodded. ''Carrots, chicken—''

''Sounds divine.''

''—liver.''

''Then again, maybe not,'' Fran amended on a chuckle.

Max stood within inches of her, the heat from his long, powerful body saturating her good sense, his gaze moving over her face, then finally settling on her eyes. ''How does cheese, fresh-baked bread and some famous Llandaron smoked oysters sound?''

Frustratingly breathless, Fran managed to squeak out, ''As opposed to the liver?''

Another smile tugged at his mouth. ''You've been

with Glinda all morning, Doctor. Don't you think she'll be all right on her own for a short while?''

''I suppose. And as a matter of fact, I have some reading I need to catch up on.'' She tried not to breathe in his scent—that amazing masculine spicy scent he wore so well. But fighting the inevitable seemed useless. ''It's a very interesting book, actually—canine lick granuloma.''

He nodded and said with mock solemnity, ''Well. I don't know if I can compete with that.''

''Do you have any information to offer on the effectiveness of drug therapy over the use of restraint collars?''

''All I have to offer is a little tour of Llandaron, maybe a picnic by the ocean and afterward a visit to Gershin's Taffy Shop.''

Her eyes went wide and her mouth watered. ''Gershin's Taffy Shop?'' It was the shop she'd read about in her guidebook—seen pictures of. The quaint little shop with its redbrick front and white-icing windows looked like something out of a Norman Rockwell painting.

''Interested?''

Fran sighed. She was lost here, utterly trumped. God and the devil were conspiring against her. They wanted to bring down the rational, realistic Dr. Charming and force her to embrace these flights of fancy.

Of course she was interested in what Prince Perfect was offering. Everything he'd suggested sounded wonderful. But what accompanied this good time in Llandaron? More warm glances, clever banter, more longing for this attraction, this loss of control that seemed to overwhelm her whenever he was near to come to fruition?

How in the world was she supposed to control an attraction that seemed uncontrollable? Perhaps recall her last experience with an irresistible heartbreaker?

Fran glanced up into blue fire and firmly said, "No, I don't think I'm interested."

"Something tells me you think too much, Doctor."

At such an acute observation, Fran dropped her gaze and returned to the comfort and safety of Glinda. Still, her curiosity got the better of her. "May I ask why you're doing this, Highness? I'm not really a guest here or anything—just a paid employee." Needing something to do, she scooped up the already full water bowl and marched over to the sink. "I mean, don't you have work to do?"

"I always have work to do," he answered dryly. "Like you, I could work all the time."

Dumping the clean water out, she expelled a breath. "What if Glinda needs something? Needs me?"

"I'll have Charlie call my cell phone if there's a problem." Like any self-respecting Type A, he had an answer for everything. "But there shouldn't be," he continued. "She's not due for a week, right?"

"Right, but—"

"No buts. It's only a couple of hours."

She bit her lip as she refilled the bowl with fresh water. He wasn't about to take no for an answer, but heck, if she really wanted to be honest with herself, she didn't want to say no.

"Francesca, you're in an enchanted land." She looked over at him; challenge lit his eyes. "You're keen on choices. Make the choice to enjoy your time here, to embrace it for once, not hide from it."

She placed the bowl in front of the wolfhound. "Look, Max, I don't know what you think you know about me, but I don't hide—"

"Glad to hear it." With a grin playing about his sensual lips, he offered her his arm like a character out of a historical-romance novel. "Car's packed. Shall we go?"

Inside her, excitement roared like a lioness with a chance to be set free from her cage for a few hours. But Fran wouldn't let Prince Max see that thrill of anticipation. For goodness' sake, the man already had too much power as it was. Instead, she shot him a withering glance, then walked past him out of the office, muttering in mock irritation, "Royal types. Always used to getting their own way."

To seduce the lovely Francesca Charming, Maxim thought, pulling his car into a parking space, he needed to tug off those custom-fit infrared sunglasses she'd bragged about wearing and allow the woman to see the rosy glow of his island nation.

He'd left the limousine at home, opting for a more relaxed way to see Llandaron—in the vintage cherry-red Mustang he and one of his father's guards had worked on for an entire summer when he was twenty-one. Maxim had never taken a woman for a ride in his car. After all, the 1965 Ford Mustang convertible was sacred. But then again, this woman was going to save him from a miserable future, so he'd made an exception.

And hell, she looked amazingly good in the convertible, her blond hair whipping against her cheeks, that irreverent laugh coating the salty breeze, as Maxim sped down crooked Terrin Lane.

"Don't you need…bodyguards or something?" Fran asked as Maxim opened the passenger door to let her out.

"They're here," he assured her.

She glanced around. "Where?"

"Keeping their distance—" he grinned "—as I requested."

"Ah. Now do they just guard your body?" she asked, stepping onto the sidewalk. "Or any and all bodies that accompany you?"

He chuckled and offered her his arm again. "They guard mine, and I guard yours."

"Why doesn't that make me feel safe?" A pretty blush crept over her cheeks as she looped her arm through his.

Surrounded by shops, several small hotels and a few touristy horse-and-carriages, Maxim and his guest were right out in the open—a deliberate action, in fact, the news of which would surely get back to his father. It didn't take long for the people in downtown Llandaron to notice him.

But no jaws dropped. There was no staring or ogling. And that was because Maxim was no stranger here. He often went to town, maybe had a beer with the locals in the pub. They were good company, and when he was with them, he felt a grain of the freedom he craved.

"Come to town often, do you?" Fran whispered.

"This is real life to me, Francesca."

"No castles, no servants, no edicts…"

"Exactly." He reached for and held her hand, heard her breath catch, saw the eyes of several passersby dart toward their entwined hands and grinned.

Fran cleared her throat. "Well, they obviously love to see you. The monarchy must be very important here."

"You have no idea how important."

Nearby, an elderly fruit vendor caught sight of them and dropped her entire box of apples. Without further thought, Maxim was on his hands and knees, picking up the fruit. Perhaps all the townspeople weren't as used to seeing him as he thought. Or maybe it was the woman at his side.

"Oh, Your Highness, you needn't…you really shouldn't," the woman sputtered.

"Nonsense." Maxim had all the apples picked up and returned to the box within minutes. The woman thanked him profusely as onlookers watched and whispered.

Francesca, on the other hand, merely smiled.

"Why do you look at me that way?" he asked as they crossed the street where the scents of sugar and vanilla and cocoa were thick in the air.

"Just impressed, Your Highness."

Suddenly Fran paused, breath held. Maxim glanced at her and saw pure, childlike excitement gleaming in those tawny eyes. She was staring at the window of Gershin's Taffy Shop.

"Look," she whispered excitedly, pointing at the two men pulling a thick wad of dark taffy. "I've got to do that," she said, then raced into the shop.

Before Maxim had time to register what she'd said—and more importantly what she planned to do—Francesca was standing in the window beside the two taffy pullers. She spotted him and waved. He grinned, shook his head and watched as she replaced one of the pullers. Like a pro, she stretched and stretched the ribbons of taffy, and laughed with the patrons watching from the inside of the shop.

Admiration filled Maxim. Admiration and envy. Granted, the people of Llandaron respected him, welcomed him into their town with a smile and into their pub for a pint, but never had he, nor could he, muck around with them.

He was their prince, not their playmate.

"Who's the girl, Highness?"

Maxim glanced over his shoulder. Garbed in something close to rags stood Ranen Turk. Going on seventy, the old friend of his father's could well afford silk and a large house by the sea, but he chose homespun cotton and an old brick town house in the heart of the village.

"She's the vet from America," Maxim supplied as he and Ranen stepped away from the window and into the freshly watered alleyway beside Gershin's.

"Taking the vet to town, are you?" Ranen's eyes narrowed. "I've never heard of you taking a lass to town before."

"She's caring for the king's wolfhound."

The old man cackled. "She's a beauty."

Maxim nodded, his lips twitching with amusement.

Ranen quickly sobered. "Well, I don't like her. I don't like her and I don't like Americans." He whipped off his tam and thwacked it against his leg, sending showers of dust into the air. "Still can't believe you didn't trust me with that dog." He shook his head. "Had to bring in a foreigner."

"The king wanted a specialist, Ranen, and you bloody well know it."

"I *am* a specialist."

Maxim smiled. "With pigs, horses, goats, chickens."

"Tosh," the man grumbled. "I tell you I don't like—"

"They gave us five whole pounds of taffy, Max!" Francesca loped into the alleyway toward him. Her eyes shone with happiness, as though she'd just been given gold bricks and not just some sweet confection. "Okay, normally I don't eat sugar or white flour or starchy vegetables, for that matter, but they were so nice and this taffy is so good, I just couldn't—"

Ranen let out a loud snort.

Francesca suddenly realized Maxim wasn't alone. "I'm so sorry. That was incredibly rude of me." She smiled at the old man. "Hello there. I'm Fran."

The man rolled his eyes.

"Francesca," Maxim said quickly, "this is Ranen Turk, our town veterinarian."

"Animal overseer," Ranen corrected. "With all

the animals apart from dogs, it seems. I'm not a real doctor like you, miss. Learned everything from doing."

"Life is the best teacher, I believe." Francesca grabbed the man's hand and shook it enthusiastically. "It's wonderful to meet you, Dr. Turk."

"Wish I could say the same, miss."

"Ranen, what the hell!" Maxim was outraged.

After such an atrocious insult, Maxim expected Francesca to blush, say nothing, maybe make an excuse to return to the taffy shop—anything to get away from the old man.

But she didn't. Hell, she smiled at him. "You know, Mr. Turk, you remind me a lot of my grandfather."

He harrumphed. "How's that?"

"Well, he was handsome, highly intelligent—" she lowered her voice "—and one very lovable pain in the ass."

A grunt escaped Maxim's throat. He glanced over at Ranen. The man's mouth was open, but nothing was coming out. After a moment, the corners of that mouth began to curve into something resembling a grin.

"I could be wrong about this one, Highness," Ranen said to Maxim.

Francesca smiled. "Well, thank you, Dr. Turk."

The old man's brow lifted. "I only said *could* be wrong, lass. Don't go telling the weekly rag."

Amusement lit her eyes. "I promise to keep your uncertain opinions of me to myself." She eyed him earnestly. "I know you're probably incredibly busy, but I would love to talk to you about the animals here in Llandaron. I bet you know everything there is.'' Then she leaned in and whispered, ''Do you know that you have very wise eyes, Dr. Turk?''

''Yes, I've heard that many times.'' Wriggling his tam back on his head, he added, ''You're welcome to stop by and see me if you're in town again.'' He thrust out a grimy hand. ''And it's Ranen.''

''Fran,'' she repeated, taking his hand.

The man everyone sent their animals to, but rarely touched because he always looked as though he'd gotten out of bed and rolled in the dirt to start his day, actually showed a few teeth with his grin as he grasped Francesca's hand.

Maxim shook his head. The town curmudgeon was falling for her. The woman had charms she didn't even know she possessed.

And God help him, he couldn't wait to explore each and every one.

Fran watched the waves slam against the rocky shoreline, greedy to possess one more inch of beach. She understood the water's need. She'd only spent a few hours in the magical little town, but it was the most wonderful two hours she'd spent in a long time—and the quickest. Strolling the tree-lined side-walks, she'd felt as though she possessed a child's heart, but a woman's mind. For today she had embraced everything and everyone, and found herself wanting more.

''A piece of taffy for your thoughts.''

Fran groaned at the man across from her on the

picnic blanket. "Get real. I think I've eaten at least three of the five pounds they gave us."

"They gave *you,* you mean."

She smiled, shook her head. A satin summer breeze wafted around them, then calmed. They were situated several feet above a private stretch of beach, on a grassy spot under an ancient maple with creamy-white leaves. Prince Max had chosen a perfect spot for a picnic—and a perfect spot for romance, if that was a consideration. Which, she had to believe, it was not. The man was an actual prince, for heaven's sake. Sure, he acted like a normal person, but he wasn't. And she refused to think of him otherwise.

No matter how easy it would be to tumble into that trap.

Leaning back against the base of the tree, Max took a bite of the cold chicken leg in his hand. "My people really like you, Francesca."

"And I like them. Especially Ranen." With a weighty sigh, Fran gathered her knees to her chest and stared out at the sea. "Are you and he close?"

"My father was an only child. He was incredibly lonely for a playmate—until he met Ranen." Max paused, and glanced out at the ocean. "Even as a young man, Ranen worked with farm animals. He would come to the palace to check on an ailing cow or a chicken that wasn't laying. After he'd finished his work, he and my father would hang around with each other until dusk. They became inseparable. To this day, they still have a Sunday-night card game."

"And what is Ranen to you?"

"To me, he is as close to an uncle as I'll ever see." His sigh was a touch plaintive. "After my mother died, he helped us all recover. He's a good man. He's family."

Thoughtfully, Fran nibbled away at her own piece of chicken. Even though she wanted to know, and know him, she wouldn't ask about his mother, how she'd died, or how it had affected him. Such information was none of her business. So she changed the subject. "It's so different here than in L.A."

"How so?"

"Well, besides the obvious lack of pollution, traffic and attitude, everyone seems to know everyone and care about everyone. It's like a...well, a family."

"You sound like Catherine."

Every muscle in Fran's body tensed. Who was Catherine? Jealousy was something Fran avoided at all costs. Max was a gentleman, he had taken her on a tour—those things did not add up to romantic interest. And even if by some inconceivable chance they did, she couldn't allow herself to succumb. But still, she had to know about the woman. "Who's Catherine?"

"My sister."

"Oh." She heaved an inward sigh of relief, and when Max grinned, she blushed.

"So you have a brother and a sister?" she said, abandoning her chicken for a vegetable pasty.

"Yes."

"Do they live here?"

"My brother and his wife live in the palace, but they're in Japan now."

"Taking in the sights?"

"Visiting the emperor."

"That was going to be my second guess."

Max chuckled. "My sister is on tour. Visiting hospitals, raising funds for several charities."

"Oh, a real go-getter, huh?"

He raised a brow. "You have no idea."

Fran laughed. "I'd love to meet her."

"She's due to visit California at the beginning of summer." He grabbed a napkin. "Perhaps then."

"Maybe." Just the thought of leaving Llandaron made her heart dip. Her appetite all but gone, she put down the vegetable pasty and mentally sighed. Crazy. She was going crazy. Either that or this place and its handsome prince had cast a spell over her.

"Thinking about Darren?"

She tossed him a grim look. "It's Dennis."

"Right."

"Actually, I was thinking about this country of yours. Such beauty is almost staggering." She smiled. "You know?"

He gaze fell to her mouth. "Yes, I do know."

Awareness rippled through her. She was no wanton creature, no seeker of pleasure, but around Max every second thought she had was improper. Maybe not for a regular guy and girl, but for an almost-engaged woman and a prince... If she could, she'd wash her mind out with soap. "We should probably pack it in."

Max didn't move a muscle. "Have you kissed this Derek, Francesca?"

Heat pulsated low and deep, but she managed a very stern, "It's Dennis."

His eyes searched hers. "You didn't answer my question."

"That's because it's none of your business."

"True."

She nodded, the butterflies in her stomach getting seasick from all the churning around. "We should really get go—"

Fran never finished the sentence. She suddenly found herself on her back, the scratchy wool blanket tickling her neck, her blood running hot and pumping fast—and her body covered by the heat of one sexy prince.

Unsure, and filled with a need she couldn't control, Fran stared up at Max, her mind hazy. His mouth was a mere breath away. His large, warm hands cupped her face. And that gaze. She shivered, forgetting who she was, forgetting who she belonged to. Passion glistened in Max's eyes, and against her hip she felt him, hard and hot.

Short, uneven breaths escaped her as she waited, wanting, *needing* him to cover her mouth with his. And finally, when she closed her eyes, she felt what she longed to feel: his lips, hot and hungry, easing down upon hers. He teased and tormented her lips with small, seductive darts of his tongue until she finally opened for him.

Her bones went liquid as he invaded her mouth, exploring in slow, velvet strokes. Heat erupted in her belly, and she wrapped her arms around his neck, her fingers thrusting into his thick hair.

Lost, so lost in feeling and sensation, she moaned into his mouth, said something like, "Max, please," and ground her hips into his erection.

A guttural groan surged from his throat, and he raised himself off her. Through a foggy haze of desire, Fran saw him hovering over her, his hands planted on either side of her body, his jaw tight, his eyes brimming with desire.

"I've wanted to do that from the first moment I saw you, Francesca."

Her limbs quivered, her voice, too. "To be honest, so have I."

Her mind warred with her need. At that moment, there was nothing she wanted more than him. But he was not for her by any stretch of the imagination.

He had a country to rule, and the only time she'd worn a crown was a paper one at a birthday party when she was a kid, for heaven's sake. They were worlds apart. She belonged in Los Angeles, at the clinic with Dennis.

She stared up at him. "I can't hang out with you anymore, Max."

"Why not?"

"You know why not." She expelled a breath. "For the next two weeks, until I leave, I have to stay away from you."

"Two weeks," he repeated, a slow, seductive smile tugging at his mouth. "You and I won't make it two days."

A shocked gasp escaped her throat just as a loud buzzing erupted from his jacket. He sat back on his heels, then dug in his pocket and pulled out a cell phone.

"What?" he said tersely. Then his gaze flickered to Fran, and his tone softened. "We'll be right there."

"What's wrong?" Fran asked, sitting up.

"We have to go. Glinda's gone into labor."

Four

The clock on the stable wall chimed twelve times. Midnight. Heating pads tucked under one arm and several blankets under the other, Maxim headed down the hall and back into the office—or what Francesca called the whelping area.

What Charlie had assumed was labor this afternoon had merely been the dog's nesting and digging. But the stable hand had been right to interrupt their picnic, no matter how frustrating it had been to cut short such an incredibly sweet encounter. But that wet and wild kiss surely wouldn't be their last. That was if Maxim had his way—and he usually did.

He paused in the doorway of the office, his gaze on the beautiful vet as she sat cross-legged on the floor beside the extra-large whelping box. The way she'd kissed him today, with her back on the blanket, her breasts pressed against his chest, the moment had been almost carnal.

Maxim recalled her quick rebuff and grinned. Francesca Charming could deny the need that ached inside her for only so long before all concerns of societal appropriateness disintegrated.

Heat swirled low in his belly as images of her filled his mind's eye. Those beautiful full lips, those tawny eyes, places where a man could get lost.

A snore rumbled from one side of the office. Maxim's father lay asleep in a chair by the wall, his head flung back. The sight had Maxim shaking off his thoughts and resuming his job as veterinary assistant. Several hours ago, Francesca had told him he didn't have to stay; she could handle whatever came her way. But Maxim had insisted. He wanted to watch her work. Wanted to watch her, period.

He walked up beside her and whispered, "How is she?"

"She's straining a bit. But it comes and goes. Her temperature has dropped, so I'd say we're close."

Glinda looked restless and confused, yet, oddly grateful that Francesca sat beside her. With her blond hair pulled back off her face, shirtsleeves pushed up, Francesca stroked the wolfhound's belly, cooing softly, reassuring the dog that she would be all right, that her babies were coming soon and when they did, she was going to be a wonderful mother.

"Do you expect any complications?" he asked, crouching beside her.

She released her hand from Glinda's stomach. "It's my job to expect anything and everything,

Highness. Wolfhounds can have a long, tricky time of it.''

Surrendering the blankets and heating pads to the small table behind her, he nodded. ''Have you delivered many litters?''

''Only when there's a problem and the mother can't do it on her own.'' She held up her hands, waggled her fingers. ''Don't worry. If that's the case, the king has hired a set of very competent hands.''

''Yes. I know.'' Impulsively, Maxim reached out, laced her small fingers with his large ones. ''Competent and beautiful hands.''

Her eyes flitted up to meet his. And though her expression was one of professional detachment, her eyes burned tawny fire.

Quick as a cat, she stole her hand back, her gaze returning to Glinda. The wolfhound took that moment to stand, step out of the box and walk around. After a few moments, she returned and lay back down again. Her panting increased, as did her look of discomfort. Then suddenly she released a low whimper.

Behind them, the king came awake with a snort. ''How is she, Doctor?''

''She's straining again, Your Highness,'' Francesca told him.

Maxim glanced sideways at her. ''Is that good?''

''It is if she keeps it up.''

For the next ten minutes, they all watched in silence as the wolfhound continued to pant heavily. Standing, lying down again, turning.

Then, like a small ocean wave, the lower half of her body contracted.

"Here we go." Francesca's voice was cool and calm. "Let's all give her space, quiet, no interruptions. Let's see if she can do this on her own."

Maxim sat on the floor in front of his father's chair. He'd seen foals being born, calves, as well. But the sight never ceased to amaze him. And he wondered for a moment if someday he, too, would be a part of bringing a new life into the world, a life he'd helped to create.

But his query was lost in the miracle of birth. Glinda pushed, moved, then pushed again. Then finally, the first pup appeared.

"Perfect position," Francesca informed them before turning back to Glinda and whispering, "You're doing great, girl."

Instinct continued to guide Glinda, until the dark, encased pup slipped out. Immediately Francesca broke the sack, made sure the pup was breathing, then laid it in front of Glinda. The new mother set about unwrapping, cleaning her baby, vigorously licking the newborn's pink face.

Francesca glanced over her shoulder at the king. "A girl, Your Highness."

"She's…just beautiful."

Maxim swore he heard tears in his father's voice. But he didn't look behind him. Neither one of them wanted to acknowledge their more tender emotions.

After about twenty minutes, Glinda's contractions began anew. The room fell silent out of respect for the dog's labor. Pup two was born, then thirty minutes later, Pup three, followed by Pups four and five. Three boys and two girls—all gray like their mother, and all healthy.

The king didn't speak, and Maxim could do nothing but stare as Glinda cared for each successive pup just as tenderly as she had the first.

"One more, sweet girl," Francesca cooed to the exhausted wolfhound.

Thirty minutes later, contractions hit Glinda again. But this time, after a few bouts of pushing, the wolfhound seemed to give up. The puppy crowned, but that was it.

Glinda looked at Francesca, confused, fearful.

Nervous energy filled the space.

But true to her word, the doctor was ready. She placed her hands on Glinda's belly, applied pressure.

"What are you doing?" Maxim asked.

"She's worn-out. I'm trying something, helping nature along a little." With great care, she kneaded Glinda's belly like bread dough, all the while talking to her softly.

Maxim watched with admiration and relief as the wolfhound seemed to understand what was required and pushed the pup all the way out. There was a collective sigh of relief. Then everyone started breathing normally as Francesca opened the sack and cleaned off the pup.

But relief was premature.

Something was wrong. The pup was pink, but totally limp. Maxim heard Francesca curse under her breath.

"What is it?" the king asked anxiously.

Francesca grabbed a warm towel. "He's not breathing."

She was infinitely gentle as she held the pup and explained to Glinda what she needed to do.

At first, Francesca cleaned the pup's nostrils with a syringe, then rubbed its belly, back and sides between the towel.

His gut tight, Maxim watched her work. He'd never seen anyone so intent, so focused. The surety of her movements, the calm in her voice as she urged the puppy to breathe.

She amazed him.

Anxious seconds ticked by, and still she continued. Maxim didn't look back at his father. He knew what he would see—a reflection of his own alarm.

Suddenly the pup opened its mouth and squeaked as it took in air. Both Maxim and his father sighed, while Francesca continued to rub and coo as the little animal cried. After several minutes, she placed the pup next to Glinda's chest, guided him to a pink nipple. Everyone watched as the newborn began to suckle.

Slowly, Francesca turned to look at both Maxim and his father, her eyes bright. "Four boys and two girls, Your Highness."

"You deserve a medal, Doctor." The King inhaled deeply. "Thank you. I was afraid he wouldn't…" He didn't finish.

Francesca nodded, smiled. "He's a tough little guy."

His chest tight, Maxim looked into those shining

eyes. Damn, she was beautiful. Beautiful and intelligent and fearless. "You saved his life, Francesca."

Two pink spots appeared on her cheeks. "I was just doing my job."

"You did more than that." The vehemence in his voice surprised him.

"Bloody right," his father said, standing up and stretching. "Let me know if there are any problems, Doctor. Again, I thank you." He smiled down at Glinda and the pups, then inclined his head at Maxim and Francesca. "Good night."

"Good night, Your Highness."

"Good night, Father."

When the king left, Maxim leaned forward and brushed a strand of hair out of Francesca's eyes. "You weren't exaggerating about your connection with animals."

Startled by his touch, she sat back, her gaze falling to her lap. "No, I wasn't." Then she turned and focused on Glinda and the suckling pups.

Maxim was undeterred by her reticent behavior. He knew the heat that simmered beneath her cool surface. She fascinated and attracted him more with every moment he passed in her company. And he was determined to break down this wall she'd built around herself, make her toss aside that absurd vow to stay away from him.

But for now, he sat beside her in silence, in respect, and observed the bonding rituals of the newest additions to the Llandaron clan.

Later that night, Fran set out fresh water and a bowl of cottage cheese, though Glinda looked uninterested in both. She lay in her box, calm as a lake on a windless day. It was Fran who felt the urge to continue doing. She was still keyed up, her body ready in case a problem should arise. Though she doubted one would.

It had to be nearly 4 a.m. Most everything and everyone slept, including the newborns. Glinda yawned broadly, closed her eyes, then opened them again, partway, as though she were testing sleep. Finally she, too, gave in.

"How's our lucky guy?"

Fran's head shot up. The prince walked toward her carrying a large brown bag, concern lighting his eyes.

"He looks good. Really good."

Max glanced down, smiling at Mom and pups, safe in their bed. Soon after the birth, Charlie had come in and put soft padding, custom fit of course, around the whelping bed.

"They look all tuckered out." Max raised an amused brow. "To use one of your American idioms."

She grinned. "That's not one of *this* American's idioms, Highness. Don't think I've ever used the word *tuckered*."

He inclined his head, ever so royally. "My mistake, Doctor."

Fran took in his casual appearance. Faded jeans—faded in all the right places—and a loose-fitting black shirt. The day before at the beach, she'd told him she couldn't spend time with him anymore. This attraction between them was foolish and complicated, and impossible.

But the truth was, he'd made her forget. About Dennis. About her past. About reality. And that frightened her.

"Shouldn't you be in bed?" she asked.

Both dark brows lifted at that, his velvet-blue eyes showing flashes of the devil that he was. Heat rushed into her cheeks. A logical question given the time of night, but suggestive right now because of this chemistry, this hunger, they shared.

"I'm not ready for bed." He grinned. "Not yet, anyway."

She swallowed over the dryness in her throat as pings of anticipation shot through her.

He held out the brown paper bag. "I brought you some dinner."

"I'm not very hungry." Not for food, anyway, dammit! She mentally rolled her eyes.

"You need to eat."

"It's too late and…"

He held out a hand to help her up. "This isn't a suggestion, Doctor."

"Excuse me?"

He looked down his aquiline nose at her. "This is a command."

"Is that so?"

"Indeed."

"As you pointed out, I'm American. You don't hold any claim over me." She'd never felt a lie so deep in her belly. A flash of Max completely naked and hovering over her dropped into her mind. She blushed straight down to her toes. Who was she kidding? He held a serious claim over her, one she had to scrape off and discard if she wanted to leave Llandaron with any sense of pride or self-respect.

"Perhaps I have no authority in the United States," he said. "But while you're in Llandaron, I am your—"

"Lord and master?" It slipped out. Her mind on how he'd look completely naked, it had just slipped out.

She wanted to disappear.

He grinned broadly, his teeth flashing in the dimly lit office. "I was going to say boss, but I like your suggestion better."

"Your Highness, I…"

He took her hand, anyway, drawing her to her feet, then hauling her against him. "Come and eat."

They remained like that for a moment—face-to-face, body to body. Fran wanted to pull away, hide, scarf down the darn sandwich he'd brought, anything to distract her from hard planes of muscle and erotic scents of vanilla and virile male. But she didn't have to pull away. The prince did it for her.

Perhaps he'd taken seriously her expressed desire to keep distance between them. Her heart dropped an inch.

Or maybe her kiss had turned him off? Her heart dropped a little more.

He led her into the clean stall next to the office. Close enough to hear if Glinda needed her and just far enough away to keep from disturbing her and the babies. Max pulled out a roast-beef sandwich, grapes and a bottle of water.

She plopped down in the sweet-smelling hay, grabbed half a sandwich. "We're eating together way too much, Highness."

He shrugged and took the other half of the sandwich. "I like your company."

Her company? As in friendship? Was she right about the kissing thing? For, it only took one kiss, she believed, to realize if you were attracted to someone. Of course, if he wasn't attracted to her, that was a good thing, right?

Munching on the delicious roast beef and freshly baked bread, she went to war with herself. She wanted him to be attracted to her, yet she couldn't let either of them do a thing about it. He was everything she was terrified to want: gorgeous, intelligent, funny—and totally unattainable.

She went for safe conversation. "So what's it really like being a prince?"

"Fantastic, trying, educational, disappointing."

A smiled played about her mouth. "It's got its ups and downs, huh?"

"Honestly, Francesca, I feel privileged to have what I have. But when duty is called into play, things can get a little…well, challenging."

She took a handful of grapes. "Are we talking parties-and-christening-ships-kind-of-challenging here, or are we talking about getting married to the horsey-looking princess of Denmark?"

He took a moment to answer. "The latter, actually."

"Really? Are you…engaged?" Why did she have trouble saying it? Or for that matter, comprehending it? For heaven's sake, she was practically engaged herself. It was just that Max had kissed her. Why would he do something like that if he was…

She stopped herself, because if she didn't she'd have to take a long, hard look at her own involvement in that kiss.

"I'm not engaged or anything close to it." The hay crackled beneath him as he reached for a few grapes. "I've told my father that I will marry a woman of my own choosing—that is, if I ever marry."

"Don't you believe in marriage?"

"I believe in freedom, Francesca. I have yet to discover a way to have both."

His words saddened her, yet she understood his aversion. "When I was nine, I found this bird in my backyard. He was—" she laughed "—really ugly. Brown and disheveled with two missing toes. I was out in my kennel feeding the rabbits when he flew right into the place, sat right beside my hand. Totally cheeky critter. He didn't have anything really wrong with him. Maybe he was just hungry or tired. I named him Oscar and fell head over heels for him. Anyway, he stayed for three months, then one day he was gone."

Fran looked up at the prince, smiled.

He returned the smile. "And the moral of the story is…?"

"Freedom and capture are an impossible duet."

She popped a grape in her mouth. But it missed, dropped onto her ankle.

Max snatched it up. Her breath caught as she watched him roll it between his fingers, then lift it to her mouth. She licked her lips, her gaze locked on his.

"Open, Doctor."

Without hesitation, she did as he instructed. His gaze followed the grape as he rubbed it against her upper lip, then slipped it into her ready mouth. She bit down, releasing its cool sweetness into her mouth. A heavy sigh rushed out of his lungs.

Dropping her gaze, Fran quickly swallowed the grape. She and Max sat in silence for a minute. Perhaps it was the food, more likely the long night, but a deep fatigue started to wash over her. She couldn't stop the yawn when it came.

"Tired?" Max asked.

"Very."

With that, he packed up the remains of the meal and tossed the bag into a nearby garbage can. "I'll walk you back to the castle."

She shook her head. "I'm staying here tonight."

"Here, where?"

"I guess on this lovely bundle of hay. I've always wanted to sleep on a hay mattress."

He chuckled. "Don't romanticize it, Doctor. I've done it many times and it's damn uncomfor—"

"You have?"

"Yes. As a child."

"Why?"

He shrugged. "Closest thing to running away from home as I could get."

Francesca's face broke out in a grin. "Freedom."

He nodded, humor glinting in his eyes. "Freedom."

It took an internal crane to look away from him and say, "I'd better get some sleep. The pups will be up first thing."

Without a word, Max left the stall, returning seconds later with a blanket.

"You didn't have to do that," Fran said. "It's a warm night. I don't think I'll need it."

"I will." Completely sober, he lay down in the hay, put his hands behind his head and closed his eyes. "Good night, Francesca."

Fran's pulse jumped. "What do you think you're doing, Highness?"

"You're not going to stay out here all alone."

"Why not? Are there trolls who come out at night and eat unsuspecting vets or something?"

His eyes opened, dark and dangerous. "Wolves."

Awareness whirled traitorously in her belly. How in the world was she supposed to sleep next to this man feeling the way she was feeling? With her breasts tightening in response to his words, her belly warming to his quick, brusque comeback?

"Look, Highness, there is no way I'm just going to—"

He pulled her down next to him and had her fitted in the crook of his arm against one steely pec before she could catch her breath. "Just put your head on my chest and keep quiet, Doctor. We're both tired. Let's try to get some sleep."

Get some sleep? Was he serious? "More commands, Highness?"

"Shh... People and animals are trying to sleep here."

She sighed with frustration, rolled her eyes to the beamed ceiling. It was pointless to argue with this man.

Giving in and giving up, she let her head fall against his delicious chest. "What about the horsey princess of Denmark?"

"What about Donald?"

"Dennis."

He chuckled. "Sleep now, evaluate tomorrow."

What a hedonistic proposition. But sadly, one Fran readily embraced with this 180-pound hunk of yummy prince beside her.

Her eyes drifted shut, and with the scents of hay and vanilla lulling her to sleep, she gave in to exhaustion.

Five

Llandaron mornings were reminiscent of a Monet.

With the bristle of soft hay beneath him, Maxim gazed out the window of the opposite stall. Cool, indistinct, raging with color. But the artist hadn't counted on this particular Llandaron morning. Surely if Monet had woken up with such an incredible beauty as Francesca wrapped in his arms, his work would've included far more sensual elements.

No more lakes and lily pads.

Unless, of course, the lily pads were just barely covering the hills and valleys of one Dr. Francesca Charming.

The image of a nude Francesca, damp leaves molded to her breasts, pounded into Maxim's brain, bringing his need to a dangerous level.

As though his body had sent her a signal to awake,

Francesca stirred. Her hand, which had rested by the hem of his shirt, dipped beneath the cotton fabric and moved upward. Maxim inhaled sharply, the lower half of him hardening to granite. Her fingers stopped on his pectoral, her palm over his nipple as she shifted in her sleep, draping her leg over his thigh.

He wanted to take her. Right then, right there. Strip off those jeans, roll her onto her back, ease up her shirt, cover her breast with his mouth and plunge deep inside her. If she awoke with the same heat in her eyes as Maxim felt in every muscle, every vein, maybe he'd do just that.

Francesca gave a soft sigh, followed by a lengthy stretch, her palm inching upward, the soft skin grazing his nipple. A raw groan escaped Maxim's throat, and he instinctively pulled her closer.

"Mmm…Max." She burrowed into the curve of his neck, her lips a few tantalizing centimeters from his skin, her knee brushing the ridge of his erection.

That was it. She'd said his name, for whatever reason. There was only so much a man could take.

Gently grasping her chin, Maxim kissed her softly on the lips. With a sleepy sigh, Francesca melted into him, her mouth moving over his, her body pressing into his side. Maxim tilted his head, changing angles, deepening the kiss. And she matched him, went with him, her sighs turning to hungry whimpers.

If anyone understood hunger, Maxim did. His fingers splayed, he cupped her breast, slowly kneading the ripe flesh through her blouse and bra. But this time she didn't purr, didn't whimper. She froze. Her eyes flew open. And unfortunately for Maxim there was no passion in those tawny depths, just confusion, confusion that quickly turned to unease.

He grinned. "Good morning."

She sat up, eyes wide. "Morning."

"How did you sleep?"

"Fine."

"I've heard that one-word answers tend to be indicative of sleep deprivation. Perhaps you should lie back down."

"No. I'm fully functioning."

"As am I."

Her gaze dipped to where the thin blanket covered the evidence of his need for her. She looked up, found him watching her. Heat pounded in her cheeks. But behind the embarrassment, Maxim saw her interest, her fire. A fire he fully intended to stoke. He wasn't used to being patient. He wasn't used to being challenged. Women sought him out, came eagerly to his bed.

But Francesca wasn't just any woman. And this fight for freedom that he had going with his father wasn't disappearing. So with Francesca, he would be patient.

She sat up, tried to smooth her rumpled clothing. "I should check on the puppies."

Maxim took her hand in his. "Before you go, I want to tell you how amazing you were last night." He saw her eyes widen with alarm and chuckled. "I'm talking about the birth of the pups."

"I know."

"You weren't sure." He turned her hand over and kissed the palm. "Trust me, Francesca, if something had happened between us last night, you would have remembered it.''

She snatched her hand from his and stood up. ''You are way too full of yourself, Highness.''

Grinning, Maxim fell back onto the hay, locked his hands behind his head. ''I meant what I said about your skill. I hope Dagwood knows how lucky he is—to have you in his veterinary practice, that is.''

''He most certainly does.'' She crossed her arms over her chest, her luscious upper lip puffing out. ''And for the last time, it's Dennis.''

His grin widened. She was beautiful when she got riled up. Too beautiful, too alluring. And if she didn't get out of here soon, he was going to lose all patience and find a way to get her naked and beneath him. ''Perhaps it's best that you go to Glinda and the pups now.''

She quirked a brow. ''Am I being dismissed, Highness?''

He chuckled. ''Not at all.'' Ripping back the blanket, Maxim showed her just how much he wanted her to stay. ''Would you care to come back to bed?''

Her eyes widened at his challenge. ''No...I... that's not what I meant. I was—''

''Probably for the best. I have to get going, anyway. My plane leaves in an hour. A quick roll in the hay is not what I had in mind for you and I, Francesca.''

Her cheeks turned bright red, and she didn't ask him what he did have in mind. ''Where are you going?''

"Paris."

"Oh? For business or...pleasure?"

"Both." He smiled. "Will you miss me?"

She shook her head. "That oh-so-healthy ego of yours is showing again, Highness." And with that, she turned and walked out of the stall, calling back, "Have a good time."

He watched her go, her hips swaying provocatively as she walked. Paris seemed dull compared to what he wanted to be doing in Llandaron. But duty called. Tossing away the blanket, he stood. He'd be back by the end of the week. He'd be back—ready and willing to continue this sweet seduction of Dr. Francesca Charming.

Business or pleasure, Your Highness?

Fran rolled her eyes as she placed Glinda's empty food bowl in the sink. What a fool. Why didn't she throw a jealous fit while she was at it?

Hey, why was she feeling jealous at all? In a week and a half, she'd be back home in L.A., back to real life and real men—not sexy princes who lived in lighthouses, charmed the socks off every woman they saw and made skeptical hearts believe that fairy tales might actually exist.

She glanced down at Glinda, who rested contently with her babies. A sense of peace blanketed Fran. She'd done exactly what she'd come here to do. Glinda had delivered well. She was eating healthy portions of her scrambled eggs and cottage cheese. All the pups were healthy and suckling. Even Fran's little miracle, number six, whom she'd aptly named Lucky.

She had a nice chunk of money for her surgery facility. She could leave with no regrets.

Her right hand tingled—the hand that had stroked Max's chest. The warmth, the strength she'd felt there had nearly turned her bones to liquid. Admittedly, she was incredibly attracted to him. And if the steel she'd felt against her thigh was any indication, she was safe to assume that Maxim was just as attracted to her.

But she couldn't even contemplate starting something up with him—no matter how strong the pull. There was Dennis, there were her feelings about smooth talkers, and then there was the fact that he was royalty!

Only one answer remained. She had to fight this attraction with everything she possessed.

Thank God he was going to Paris. It would make resisting him much easier. Perhaps he would stay away until it was time for her to leave.

Tonight she would call Dennis. They'd have a nice long talk. And over the next few days, she'd immerse herself in her work and forget all about His Highness.

Well, she'd try, anyway.

"Five days old and growing like weeds, they are."

Francesca smiled into the eyes of Ranen Turk, who had come to the castle for a formal dinner party with the king, but had stopped off at the stables to see the pups. The old curmudgeon really did remind her of her grandfather. Boorish on the outside, a big teddy bear on the inside. And because he reminded her of her grandfather, she couldn't help thinking of her father. Which made her heart hurt.

She sat down on the chair beside Ranen, gestured toward the whelping box with her chin. "They're sure going to keep Glinda busy."

"The cost of becoming a mum, miss."

"A mum with sextuplets."

"I hear wolfhound litters can run to fifteen or more."

"That's true. So I guess six for her is like one for a human mother." She was silent a moment before asking, "Do you think she's too thin?"

"No, no. She looks just right." He turned to Fran. He didn't smile, and his eyes narrowed. "But something tells me you already knew that."

She shrugged, grinned. "I wanted a second opinion."

"Did you, now?"

"Yes. Any crime against that?" Her grin widened.

He scratched his beard, specks of dust flicking into the air. "Not altogether certain. I'll have to check and see if there's a law against butter'n up an old goat."

Fran couldn't help herself. She threw her head back and laughed. "Are you sure you and my grandfather aren't long-lost brothers?"

It felt good to laugh. The past few days hadn't been as easy as she'd hoped. She'd only spoken to Dennis twice, and each time he'd had to run after about five minutes. And then there was the real trouble: Max. Perhaps if she'd had more work to do, more patients to look after, her mind would have been more occupied.

But she didn't and it wasn't. She'd been hired to care for Glinda and the pups, and that left a lot of daydreaming time. And not only did Max invade her thoughts during the day, but he came to her at night. Silky, sweaty dreams that had her waking in dual hope and panic that he was back home and in her bed.

"Are you coming along to supper this evening?"

Fran's gaze traveled over the old man's evening attire. He looked far better suited to a sheep-shearing festival than a dinner party at the palace. But whatever, he was a rule breaker, an individualist, and she liked that.

She shook her head. "I don't think so."

"Why not?"

"Little uncomfortable, I guess. I'm just plain old Fran Charming from Southern California. The whole royal scene isn't right for someone like me."

"Hog slop."

She lifted a finger. "*And* I don't really know anyone."

"You know me." He lowered his chin and gave her a somber glare. "And you know His Highness."

"I don't really know the king, Ranen."

"I didn't mean *that* Highness, lass."

Her pulse pounded in her ears like a bedside alarm clock. "But the prince is in Paris."

Ranen shook his head. "Not anymore. Rang his father this morning. Should be back in Llandaron by the start of the fog."

Could the old man hear the thud of her heart?

He watched her closely. "Does this change your mind about supper?"

"I'm not sure." She sounded so…indecisive, timid. What was the matter with her?

"I'll tell one of the servants to come fetch you at half-past seven. The king will want to toast you in front of his guests after saving the pup the way you did." With a wink, he ambled out of the stables, muttering something along the lines of, "Should prove a right entertaining evening."

Leaning back in her chair, Fran assessed the situation. Her heart was excited, her mind wary. She had six days left here. If she could hardly fill her days, what was she going to do with the nights?

Read? Take a hot bath, stay in bed? Try to call Dennis again?

She looked at Glinda and could have sworn the dog rolled her eyes.

Fran smiled at her. "You said it, sweet girl. I'm just walking through the fire begging to get burned."

Laughter and lively conversation filled the spacious dining room, making Maxim long for the invisibility of the fog outside. He'd been back in Llandaron for all of thirty minutes, and his father was already parading prospective brides in front of him.

After a healthy swallow of whiskey, Maxim excused himself and left the side of a garrulous duchess and her beaming mother. The fire in the marble fireplace was far more appealing. He should have suspected something when his father notified him about this dinner with "a few friends."

Maxim had expected Ranen and Father Tom, not half the bloody court.

And where was Francesca?

He needed her beside him—keeping his father in check, making him wonder, making him see where his bulldozing ways might lead his son.

Maxim drained his glass. Who was he kidding? Seeing Francesca was about far more than just his father. Even from Paris, the beautiful veterinarian had ruled his mind. Stylish parties, equally stylish women, intensive work schedules—nothing had held his attention. Finally he'd come to realize that his attraction to Francesca was unlike any he'd ever known, and that if he didn't have her soon, she would continue to consume him. And he couldn't afford to be so preoccupied.

He had to finish what he'd begun.

Behind him, the butler announced dinner. Two by two, guests found their seats around the ancient fifty-foot-long table. Several women glanced his way, wondering if he would be seated beside them. Maxim chuckled under his breath. Little did they know that he'd already taken care of who sat beside him. He glanced at his watch. That is, if his dinner companion showed up.

The thought had barely formed when the noise level in the room dropped, and curious gazes flew to the doorway.

Five days suddenly seemed like five months to

Maxim as he took in every inch of Francesca Charming.

She was a vision, all the way down to her barely there sandals and soft-pink toenails. The white silk dress she wore, with its thin spaghetti straps and low neckline, clung to her lush curves like a lover's hands. The skirt fell just below the knee, showing off long, lightly tanned legs. Max swallowed the rush of desire that ripped through him as he forced his gaze upward. But the move only made things worse. Honey-blond waves teased her shoulders and framed her face. A face made impossibly more beautiful with flawless makeup, tawny eyes and lightly glossed lips.

She was both saint and sinner. She made his fingers itch to touch, caress…

Depositing his glass on the mantel, he crossed to her. "You look stunning, Doctor."

She smiled. "Thank you. And may I say you look pretty stunning yourself, Your Highness?"

"You may, but only if you drop the 'Highness' for tonight. How about Maxim?" He leaned in, whispered in her ear, "Or if you can't help yourself, I'll try to be content with Max."

A soft sigh rushed from her lips, and she pulled away from his proximity. "I can always help myself." And with that, she walked straight past him and went to find her seat.

Maxim watched her go, his senses keen, still reeling from that delectable fragrance she wore. Spicy floral. Intoxicating as hell.

As everyone found their place cards, Maxim wan-

dered over to the table. All eyes were on him as he
pretended to look for his own card. Normally he sat
opposite his father, but tonight the old man had instructed the housekeeper to put his son between two
available females.

A footman pulled out Francesca's chair and she
sat down next to Ranen.

"Well, look at this." The same footman held out
the chair of the vacant seat on her other side. Maxim
sat down. "We've been seated next to each other."

"Look at that," she said dryly.

A gruff chuckle sounded from Ranen Turk. "Yes,
look at that."

The king interrupted their observations by picking
up his wineglass. "Good evening and thank you all
for coming. And a special thank-you to Dr. Charming
for her fine skill at bringing six healthy royal pups
into the world."

Francesca blushed prettily as everyone drank.
Soon food was being served and conversations
sprang to life.

Maxim turned to her. "How are the pups?"

"Perfect."

"I would have been down to see them, but I just
arrived."

"You'll have plenty of time to enjoy them. They'll
need lots of love and attention when I leave."

"And when is that?"

"Next week."

"So soon?"

"I'm afraid so."

A few feet away, his father caught his eye,

frowned. "Maxim, shouldn't you be down at the other end beside Lady Anna and Lady Elizabeth?"

Maxim held up his place card. "I am right where I belong, Father."

The king opened his mouth to reply, but Ranen took that particular moment to needle his old friend about the card game he'd lost last week.

As the staff served the first course, Maxim's gaze moved to Francesca. Though a plate of fresh greens and strawberries was placed before her, she was staring at him, curiosity behind her eyes.

"So, how was Paris? Eiffel Tower still standing?"

He grinned, picked up his salad fork. "Paris was…enlightening."

"That sounds interesting."

"It is Paris, after all. Just breathing the air is stimulating."

"Beautiful city, beautiful people."

Maxim smiled. She was covertly inquiring about his personal time in Paris. And doing a bloody poor job of it. "If you'd like to know if I spent any time with women while in Paris, all you have to do is ask."

Her breath caught. "Of course I don't want to know any such—"

"I'm perfectly comfortable discussing it."

"I'm sure you are." With an indignant lift of her chin, she picked up her fork and dug into her salad. "I think I'm going to ignore you now, Your Highness, and talk to Ranen."

"No, I don't think so," he said, amused.

"Oh, and why not?"

He glanced over her head, then back at her. "Ranen is talking to my father. You don't want to interrupt the king, do you?"

She turned back to her salad and muttered, "Dammit."

He laughed, whispered, "No cursing at the dinner table, Doctor."

This time when she glanced his way, amusement flashed in her eyes, and a smile tugged at her mouth. If he covered that mouth with his right now, would anyone notice? Perhaps they could slip under the table for a few moments and—

"Pardon me, Dr. Charming, but you have a phone call." The butler stood over them. "A Dr. Dennis Cavanaugh."

Fran felt the strawberry she'd just eaten drop like a lead ball to the bottom of her stomach. She looked at Max. His eyes were almost black. And she wondered if he was angry because she had to leave the table or because Dennis was calling.

She stood. "Excuse me."

After receiving the king's nod of dismissal, Fran left the room, feeling Maxim's eyes on her back all the way down the hall. Dennis had the number to the palace, but until tonight, he'd never used it.

The butler showed her into a small library, then left, closing the door behind him. She snatched up the receiver and sat. The leather couch dipped with her weight.

"Dennis, hello. How are you?"

"Just missing you, Frannie."

She sighed with relief and cringed with annoyance

at the same time. She didn't like being called Frannie. It always made her feel like a toy poodle.

"It's good to hear your voice," she told him. "We haven't really had much chance to talk when I've called."

"I know, I know. It's been crazy here." There was a big pause, then, "Look, Frannie, I know I told you I'd wait until you got back to L.A. to hear if you've accepted my proposal, but I just can't."

Fran bit her lip. "What exactly are you saying, Dennis?"

"I need to know now. Tonight. Are you going to marry me?"

Six

Fran placed little Lucky beside his mother, then sat back against the stable wall. Being near Glinda and the pups made her feel safe, made her feel in control. She was a top veterinarian, a professional. In this room, her life made sense.

But back at the palace, where lords and ladies discussed Llandaron politics while eating venison and pumpkin soup, things didn't make sense at all.

Sitting at that table, she'd felt out of control, yet wonderful, as though she was in the presence of something…magical.

And then there was the prince with his cobalt eyes and beautiful mouth, a mouth that could make her nuts with both speech and kiss, a mouth that had made her feel two things she hadn't felt in a very long time: desirable and all woman.

Yet she'd left. She'd told the butler that she needed to check on the pups and walked away from all those glorious feelings.

"You missed dessert."

Her head came up with a snap. Speak of the blue-eyed devil. "I'm not hungry."

With four easy strides, he walked over to her, stood above her, looking unbelievably gorgeous in his black tux. "Something wrong with Dennis?"

Her brows inched together. "Did you actually call him Dennis?"

"Well, if he's in hospital or stuck on a deserted island starving and close to madness, I don't want to seem heartless."

A smile tugged at her mouth. "That's very generous of you, Max."

"Would you like to tell me what's wrong?"

"No, not really."

He chuckled, grabbed a chair and sat down in front of her. "Spill it, Doctor."

Why had he come here? Why was he interested in her problems? Curiosity about Dennis was one thing, but to leave his father's party and all those guests, all those dazzling females who watched every move he made... She sighed.

And just because he'd asked, did she really want to share her private feelings with him? With a man who made her insides heat up faster than a stretch of blacktop on a summer afternoon in Arizona? She avoided his gaze, and muttered, "I don't know, Max."

"Come on."

"It's not really something I want to—"

"I'm a very good listener." He nodded toward the whelping box. "Just ask Glinda."

Her gaze swung to Glinda. The wolfhound looked from Fran to Max, then back again. Fran laughed. "Heard all about her aching back and swollen feet during her pregnancy, did you?"

"Exactly." A grin never looked so good on any man. "Now what's wrong?"

She took a deep breath. Perhaps it was better if he did know. Perhaps then he'd stop pursuing her. And in turn, she'd stop desperately wanting him to. "Dennis isn't just a...friend and a—"

"Good man."

"Right."

"He's your boyfriend."

"Yes. And..."

"And?" he prompted.

She gave him her best mock evil eye. "Are you going to listen or what?"

He held up both hands, amused. "I apologize. Continue."

"Okay. This is the thing. Before I left for Llandaron, Dennis asked me to marry him."

Maxim stilled. His gut tightened as every word she'd uttered replayed in his mind. He'd surmised that Francesca and this Dennis guy were dating, but he never would have guessed something like this, something as serious as an offer of marriage.

Curses rested on the tip of his tongue. One, because he didn't like the idea of her marrying anyone, much less the boring L.A. vet. And two, because he didn't like that he didn't like it.

When he found her gaze, unease resided there. An unease he shared. "And did you accept?"

"I told him I had to think about it."

"So that's why he called? To get your answer?"

After a weighty exhale, she nodded. "He says he doesn't want to wait any longer. And you know what? He really shouldn't have to."

Maxim couldn't care less about poor Dennis and his lengthy wait. "How were things left?"

"Up in the air. He got beeped with an emergency and had to get to the clinic." Her gaze fell, her tone softened. "I told him I'd call him tomorrow night."

"With an answer."

"Yes."

They sat in silence, neither wanting to face the many weighty questions and answers. Sure, Maxim wanted her to turn the American down. Not just because of the plan to get his father off his back. It was something more.

In truth, Maxim had a great deal of interest in Francesca Charming, a want, a need. But what was that? Nothing lasting. And a woman like Francesca deserved something lasting. He shouldn't try to sway her, advise her to say no to the American's offer, to his promise of a future, of a home and children. Of a normal life.

No matter how much he wanted to.

Her eyes liquid and soft, she smiled up at him, weakening his resolve.

Practicality, right and wrong, good and evil—it all faded when he was this close to her.

He took her hand, pulled her to her feet. "Come on."

"To where?"

"My place."

"No." She said the word, but she didn't drop his hand or her gaze. "That's the last place I should be going tonight, Max."

He flashed her a wicked smile. "Don't trust yourself with me, Doctor?"

"Of course I do."

"Then what's the problem?" He looked at Glinda and the pups. "Everyone's asleep."

"Don't you have a party to get back to?"

"No. My father's got everything covered." He took in her wary expression. "I had the butler bring our dessert to the lighthouse. I want to show you something."

Eyes wide, cheeks flushed, she stuttered, "I really shouldn't leave—"

"There is another American saying that I've found rather useful."

"Oh yeah? What's that?"

With a grin, he led her out of the office. "All work and no play, Doctor…"

"Chess."

The word just slid off Max's tongue like honey, Fran mused as she took in the welcoming sight before her. Beside an easy fire in the lighthouse's magnificent living room sat two comfortable-looking leather armchairs. And between them was the most beautiful chess table she'd ever seen. Made of ebony and some type of redwood, the table boasted two drawers, long tapered legs, what her father had called egg-and-dart moldings, and an inlaid chessboard built into the top.

"This is incredible," she said, running her hand across its smooth surface.

"This table was my great-great-grandfather's. A local man built it, even carved these pieces out of rosewood." He pulled a mahogany case with brass handles off the mantel, clicked it open and proceeded to place the exquisitely carved chess pieces on the board. "My father wasn't much of a player, but I'm addicted. Have been since second grade."

He took off his tux jacket, and dropped it over the back of the chair. "I thought I'd teach you and we could play a game."

"Teach me?" Fran bit the inside of her cheek to keep from laughing. Holy sexism, Batman! Teach her?

Because chess was predominantly a man's game, Max just assumed she didn't know how to play. In actuality, her father had taught her many moons ago. Today, she played on the Internet with people from all over the world—and wiped the floor with the lot of them.

But Max didn't need to know that. Not yet anyway.

She sat down opposite him, shrugged. "Let's just give it a go. I know a little, enough to get through a game." *A little* as in she'd played since she was a little girl. From the age of four, to be exact.

"Are you sure?"

"Positive." She touched a bishop, batted her eyelashes at him and asked dimly, "This is a pawn, right?"

"No, that's a…" He glanced up, eyes narrowed. "You wouldn't be yanking my chain, would you?"

She laughed gently. "Maybe a little." He wasn't fooled easily—she'd have to remember that. "And by the way, 'yanking my chain'? Where did you pick up that gem?"

"Milwaukee." He opened one of the side drawers and took out a pad of paper and a pencil. "I had a week of meetings there last year. Beer, ball games, bawdy humor. I had a great time. Very colorful people."

"I'm sure they'd be glad to hear that the prince of Llandaron thinks they're colorful," she said on a chuckle. "You really like America, huh?"

"I do. I spent a great deal of time there up…until a few years ago."

Fran watched his playful demeanor evaporate. She wondered what had happened a few years ago to keep him in Llandaron. But he didn't look at all willing to speak of the past, and Fran desperately wanted to bring back the lighthearted mood from moments ago.

She shot him a wry smile. "So, are we going to play or what?"

"We're playing." With a raised brow and a slow grin, he eased out a white pawn.

"Only one space. Interesting."

"I'm full of surprises, Doctor."

Ignoring the heat low in her belly, Fran jumped her knight. "Well, watch out, because so am I."

His gaze practically seared right through her. "I'm certainly looking forward to discovering each and every one."

Throat dry, her fingers hesitated over her pawn. He was back to his old self—with a vengeance. "Stop trying to unnerve me."

"Is that what I'm doing?"

That devil grin that held way too many promises was going to be the death of her. But not tonight. Tonight she had something to prove. Strength of will.

With a flash of zeal, she took out her queen.

"Bold, Doctor."

"Try confident, Highness."

Each move he tossed her way, Fran equaled, then surpassed, putting him on the defensive. He was a very good player, assertive, demanding. The kind of player she adored.

The fire crackled low as her rook sat perfectly positioned, his king in check. She lifted an eyebrow in his direction, feeling cocky as all get-out. But she was a fool to underestimate him. With that killer smile playing about his lips, Max pulled out stop after stop. And in under ten seconds, had her king in checkmate.

"One more game," she demanded.

He nodded, his eyes bright with aplomb. "Are you sure you can stand to lose again?"

Heat blasted into her cheeks. "Shall we put a little wager on this?"

"Like what?"

"Your piece of Llandaron sweet cake?"

"You can have my cake, Francesca. Let's wager something more difficult to part with."

As his gaze roamed over her, Fran found it difficult to breathe. "I'm going to guess you've got an idea."

"How about time."

Her brow furrowed. "Time?"

With his chin resting on his elbow and his eyes resting on her, he explained, "If I win you stay in Llandaron for another two weeks." He smiled. "To look after Glinda and her pups of course."

Her breasts tightened. Two more weeks with and around this man. "And if I win?"

"You go home as planned. Back to Los Angeles, to the clinic and to—"

"All right, all right." She understood. Back to L.A. Back to Dennis. Sadly, neither one sounded all that appealing right now. What sounded appealing was the man sitting right in front of her.

From the moment she'd arrived in Llandaron and had that battle of wits with the drop-dead gorgeous and half-naked stable hand, she'd been lost.

Perhaps found, as well.

Fran inhaled deeply, sitting up tall in her chair. She would play this game with everything she had in her and let fate decide the outcome. "Okay, Highness. Prepare yourself. You're going down."

The grin he shot her way had "wicked" written

all over it. For the second time that night, her cheeks erupted with heat. "I meant you're going to lose."

His chuckle was warm, rich. "Are you always this enthusiastic when playing games?"

"Make your move, Max."

"Don't tempt me, Francesca."

With a huff, she reached out, picked up his pawn and moved it forward a space.

"Cheater," he charged on a laugh.

"Oh, please, it's your standard move." To further drive home her point, she took her knight out. "There. We even now?"

"Yes. I'd say we are even."

Fran had never played such a fierce game in all her life. Pieces were being eaten up and spit out. Eyes remained riveted on the board. Moves didn't take more than thirty seconds. It was a true battle of wills.

But in the end, there could be only one victor.

Her pulse pounding in her ears, Fran glanced up and stared into the eyes of the man she wanted more than her next breath. "Checkmate."

Without dropping his steely gaze, Max toppled his king with his forefinger. The sound of wood hitting wood echoed through the room.

"You win, Doctor."

Fran said nothing. Because in all honesty, she wasn't sure that she really had.

His bed felt like concrete, his pillow like a marshmallow. Odd he hadn't noticed that in the twelve years he'd lived here. Perhaps it was the effects of the trip.

In Paris he hadn't gone to sleep before four in the morning. Crashing into a strange bed, exhausted after a full night's work, his mind done. But it was only eleven o'clock in Llandaron, and his mind was on her. He missed the hay. Missed her. More than his next breath, he'd wanted her to stay with him tonight. But he wasn't going to push the idea until she gave Dagwood an answer.

"Max?" The soft call was followed by an even softer knock on his bedroom door.

He was out of bed in a flash, sheet wrapped around his waist. He opened the door to a bashful-looking Francesca. The gasp she made was followed by a long perusal of his chest and the low-slung sheet.

"I'm so sorry." Her cheeks were crimson in the dim light. "This is totally inappropriate."

With his free hand, Maxim reached around, touched the small of her back and led her into the room. "Are you okay?"

"No." Without his guidance, she sat down on the edge of his bed, looked up at him.

"What is it?"

"I had to talk to you." The light from the hall illuminated her face, her liquid eyes. "I know I won the bet, but…"

"But?"

"I don't want to go. Not yet."

An invisible fist gripped his heart, squeezed. "Then don't, Francesca."

She didn't say anything, was quiet for a few mo-

If offer card is missing write to: Silhouette Reader Service, 3010 Walden Ave., P.O. Box 1867, Buffalo, NY 14240-1867

NO POSTAGE
NECESSARY
IF MAILED
IN THE
UNITED STATES

BUSINESS REPLY MAIL

FIRST-CLASS MAIL   PERMIT NO. 717-003   BUFFALO, NY

POSTAGE WILL BE PAID BY ADDRESSEE

SILHOUETTE READER SERVICE
3010 WALDEN AVE
PO BOX 1867
BUFFALO NY 14240-9952

Play the Romance Crossword Game

and get... 2 FREE BOOKS

and a FREE GIFT...

YOURS to KEEP!

Scratch Here!

to reveal the hidden words.
Look below to see what you get.

Yes! have scratched off the gold areas. Please send me my **2 FREE BOOKS** and **FREE GIFT** for which I qualify. I understand that I am under no obligation to purchase any books as explained on the back of this card.

326 SDL DRTR   **225 SDL DRT7**

FIRST NAME   LAST NAME

ADDRESS

APT.#   CITY

STATE/PROV.   ZIP/POSTAL CODE

Visit us online at
www.eHarlequin.com

ROMANCE	MYSTERY	NOVEL	GIFT
You get **2 FREE BOOKS** PLUS a **FREE GIFT!**	You get **2 FREE BOOKS!**	You get **1 FREE BOOK!**	You get a **FREE MYSTERY GIFT!**

Offer limited to one per household and not valid to current Silhouette Desire® subscribers.
All orders subject to approval.

ments. Then her eyes darkened and she reached out, touched his chest. At the feel of her fingers on his skin, Maxim dragged in a breath, the lower half of him going hard. He knew Francesca noticed, but she didn't shy away.

"Tell me again that there's no horsey-looking princess?"

"There's no one." No one but the woman sitting on his bed.

"Good." She continued her tour of his chest, grazing his skin with her palm, then raking downward with her nails. That sweet honey scent of her infused Maxim's mind. He couldn't stop his labored breathing, couldn't stop the bunching and flexing beneath her touch. Every inch of him throbbed painfully. Then, just when he thought he'd lose his mind, she drew near to the edge of the black silk sheet and paused.

He laid a hand over hers. "Stay with me tonight."

It took her a moment to answer. "I can't."

"Yes, you can."

She shook her head, her eyes the color of the mahogany chess pieces that had beaten him. "I have to go back to the castle. I told the guard I would be right back, told him I'd left my purse up here."

"Forget the guard. I'll take care of him. He won't ask you where you're going ever again."

"No. Max, please." She stood, dropped her hand from his searing flesh. "I don't want people talking." Her gaze melted his resolve. "And besides, I have a phone call that can't wait."

On a growl, Maxim backed up a foot. As much as

he hated to admit it, she was right. If they were going to enjoy these two weeks, she needed to take care of business back home.

"Tomorrow night I'm taking you out." He'd meant his words as an offer, but they came out as a husky command.

"Like a date?"

"Exactly like a date."

She smiled. "I can't wait."

Neither could he. But he'd have to.

He walked her to the door, but didn't open it. Leaning against it, he said, "I can't let you go until I know why."

"Why what?"

"Why you decided to forgo the conditions of the bet. Why you're staying in Llandaron."

With a shy smile, she moved closer and gave him a slow, drugging kiss. "That's why, Highness."

Like a dying man in search of the only thing that would sustain him, Maxim hauled her against him. His free hand cupping her sweet backside, he made love to her mouth. Heat against wet, her tongue met his as they took and gave, their kisses turning fevered.

When she finally pulled back, she was breathless, her voice husky. "Whatever is happening here between us is something I can't deny or control. And whether it runs its course in two hours, two nights or two weeks, I've got to see where—"

"I know, Francesca. I know." He covered her mouth one last time, his body so hard, so ready. And she followed his movement, pressing her hips up, against his erection. Need filled him almost to the point of pain, yet he fought himself and released her.

She would come to him freely.

He stepped away from the door, opened it. "I'll see you tomorrow."

She nodded, her cheeks flushed, her lips swollen and red.

"Go, Francesca." He turned around, faced the wall. "I swear to God I won't be a gentleman for much longer."

Senses peaked, Maxim listened as she left the room, closed the door. Then he pitched the silk sheet and headed for the bathroom and one hell of an ice-cold shower.

Fran hung up the phone, switched off the light and settled into bed, feeling equal amounts of relief, anticipation, guilt and sadness.

Dennis had been incredibly forgiving.

As he wasn't a believer in true love, he hadn't gone away with a broken heart. He had, however, gone away with a question unanswered by his ex-girlfriend. One that should've been easy to answer, but wasn't.

Why?

Turning onto her side, Fran hugged her pillow tightly. She hadn't lied to him, yet she hadn't been able to tell him the truth: that the sensible, practical, intelligent Dr. Charming had gone and done the unthinkable—she'd fallen in love with the prince of Llandaron.

Seven

―――――

"**W**hat the devil do you think you're doing, Maxim?"

"Reading the newspaper, Father." Parked in one of the library's most uncomfortable armchairs, Maxim flipped through the *Times*. "Did you know that Britain's top bureaucrats have been awarded pay increases of up to fifty percent?"

With a decided harrumph, the king replied, "No, I did not know that."

"Outrageous."

"Maxim." Warning dripped from the king's tone.

"Yes? What is it?" As if Maxim didn't already know what his father wanted. As if he hadn't come in here for just this type of interrogation.

"You are taking Dr. Charming out tonight?"

Maxim smiled behind his paper. "I'm taking her to the Llandaron fair."

Cooped up with Glinda and the pups for most of the day, Maxim thought that Francesca might enjoy some time outside in the fresh air. The fair provided the perfect blend of exposure and time. He needed to be seen with her, but far more importantly, he wanted to spend time with the most beautiful woman in his country.

For one week every year, Llandaron held a small fair. Booths selling delicious local dishes were set up all around the perimeter of the fairgrounds, while games and rides dominated the center. Maxim hadn't been to the fair in years, and it was about time he attended. Besides, he deserved a little play after working like a madman on corporate contracts all night—that is, ever since Dr. Charming left his room, left him fully awake and fully aroused.

Needless to say, the cold shower had worked about as well as a fur coat in summer.

"I don't like it, Maxim."

Maxim folded the newspaper and tossed it onto the side table. "Why is that, Father?"

"What will people think? This is the second time you've paraded her in front of the town."

"Paraded her?" He leaned forward, elbows resting on the wide arms of the chair. "Father, your classist face is showing and it's not very attractive."

Rubbing his beard, the king snorted. "You know this has nothing to do with who she is or where she's come from."

"No?"

"No."

"Then what is it?"

"Dr. Charming is beautiful, intelligent and personable. Ranen thinks the world of her and so do I."

Maxim sat back in his seat. He was getting far too irritated here. Wasn't this what he wanted? His father up in arms, worried that his son was interested in a commoner—worried enough to leap off the marriage train? "What's your point, Father?"

"Llandaroners are romantics, Maxim. They love to see their royal family happy and happily settled." He threw up his hands. "They see the two of you together and they will believe a romance is blossoming."

Maxim raised a brow. "Let them." Bloody hell, he meant it. What was wrong with him? This thing between him and Francesca wasn't about romance. It was about lust and need and want. Had to be.

"Don't be so cavalier about this, Maxim. After this sad, heirless situation with your brother, the people now look to you. When I announce your fiancée at the ball, they will feel cheated."

"You're pushing me too far, Father."

"When Dr. Charming returns to her home and her life after you've carried on with her so, how do you think people will react?"

Maxim stood up, teeth clenched. "I'm done here."

"You will disappoint them, Maxim, these people you claim to care so much about."

Frustration sank deep into his bones. It was plain to see that this father wasn't going to give up any more than Maxim was going to give in.

He did care about his people, more than he wanted to. But should he abandon his own needs for his people's well-being?

He drove a hand through his hair. He knew the answer. He'd always known it. But by God, he was going to enjoy the next two weeks. His people, his father, his country—they could have the rest of his life.

"By the way, I've invited Francesca to stay on for two more weeks." Maxim inclined his head. "Good evening, Your Highness."

The man let out a lumbered sigh. "Pray tell Dr. Charming good evening from the king."

Laughter bubbled up from Fran's throat.

Three…two…one!

With all her might, she reeled back and tossed the cream pie. She held her breath as the delectable coconut-cream concoction sailed through the late-afternoon air and landed dead center on its target with a superb *splat*.

Behind her and Max, the crowd roared with laughter and applause. All around them, merry was being made, sugar popcorn was being devoured, kids were running from one ride to the next. To Francesca, coming to the Llandaron fair had been the perfect idea, the perfect date.

A grand smile on her face, she turned to Max and whispered, "Tell me again, who's behind all that whipped cream?"

"That would be Dr. Underhill you pummeled."

"Remind me not to get sick or break a leg or something while I'm here."

"Don't worry." He leaned in, whispered in her ear, "If you break a leg, I'll carry you around."

Shivering from his warm breath and sexy promise, she couldn't help but ask, "Slung over one shoulder, right?"

He nodded, a twinkle in his eyes. "I shall carry you off to my cave."

Last night she'd dropped by his "cave." A dark, dangerous place that she wanted to visit again. Fran smoothed down her blue blouse and peasant skirt.

"How about we go right over there—" she pointed to a small food stand "—for some cheese and biscuits? It's getting close to dinnertime and I'm starved."

"All right, milady." He took her hand and kissed it. "Cheese and biscuits now…cave later."

Soft sea air brushed her cheeks, cooling the heat that dwelled there. But the breeze did little to calm the fire that raged in her. Last night and all day today, she'd thought about letting go of those inhibitions, rules and fears that held her hostage.

She wanted Max. He wanted her.

For two weeks, could she leap over those three hurdles and let herself relish this time with him?

As Max led her over to the food stand, her gaze traveled over him possessively. His tanned forearms, broad build, powerful shoulders, tapered waist and incredible backside all shown off to their best advantage in jeans and a black shirt, cuffs rolled up. And that face, chiseled and so sensual. Her body hummed in remembrance. His lips on hers. His strong hands cupping her backside as he pulled her close. His eyes watching her as she touched his bare chest.

She was lost in her need for him. And she prayed to God that no one found her—at least for a little while.

"Two of everything," she heard Max tell the young blonde behind the stand's two-by-four counter.

The girl smiled coyly. "Anything else, Your Highness?"

"No, that will be all."

If Fran had been raised differently, she might've flung herself over the counter and decked the cheeky girl. But as jealousy had never ruled her head before, she wasn't about to let it run things now. She may be over the moon for the prince, but she wasn't completely off her rocker. And besides, she had no claim on him.

As they ate their cheese and biscuits and lemonade at a nearby picnic table, Fran couldn't help but notice how people watched them. With real interest, coy smiles, whispers. And to make matters worse—or better, depending on how you looked at it—after she and Max finished their snack, he made an even bigger display by taking her hand as they walked toward the rides and games.

Had he ever walked hand in hand with a woman in front of his people? she wondered. And if so, who was she and when had they known each—

"Highness, Francesca. Over here."

The enthusiastic call of Ranen Turk interrupted her thoughts. She turned toward his voice. Bracketed by the always popular ring-toss booth and the almost impossible balloon-dart booth was a large red platform. On it was a sort of scale with a bell at the top.

The sign read: FEATS OF STRENGTH. Ring the Bell. 3 Tries to win a Prize.

"What do we have here?" Max said on a chuckle as they crossed to the platform. "Manning the strong-arm booth, are you, Ranen?"

"Aye." Wielding a huge mallet, Ranen Turk sauntered forward, eyeballing Max. "Think you got it in you, Highness?"

"Maybe later."

"We just ate," Fran supplied, hearing her stepmother's loud cackle as she warned her "real" children about the dangers of physical exercise directly after eating.

"Getting soft in your old age, Highness?"

Maxim shook his head, grinning. "You really are an ass, Ranen."

"Rather an ass than a turtle." A crowd was beginning to form, curious about this battle of words.

"He wants a show," Maxim muttered to Fran. "And he won't let up until he gets one. I wanted to take you on a ride. I suppose it will have to wait." Before jumping up on the stage, he turned back to Fran. "How about a kiss for luck?"

Her cheeks burned. "There are people around."

Amusement lit his eyes. "Are you ashamed to be seen with me?"

"Get real. I'm trying to protect *your* reputation, not mine."

His gaze fixed on hers, he reached around, cupped the back of her neck. "My reputation was ruined long ago, Doctor." Without waiting for a reply, he covered her mouth with his. Just a soft kiss, nothing too intense, but damned if Fran didn't feel it everywhere.

When he released her, he bounded up onto the platform. Fran kept her eyes forward. No way was she checking to see how many people were staring at her, wondering things she herself didn't dare wonder.

Thankfully, Max took all the attention on himself, holding the mallet above his head in a great show, calling out to the growing crowd, "Long live Llandaron."

"Long live, Prince Maxim," they shouted in return.

Maxim raised the mallet, the muscles in his arms straining, then swung. When it hit the metal, up went the meter. Up, up to just inches below the bell. The crowd groaned. Ranen grinned. Maxim put up a hand, willing them all into silence.

Again he raised the mallet, swung...whack.
The meter shot up. This time, he missed the bell by a hair. Sweat glistened on his brow.

"Ready to give in, Highness?" Ranen chided.

"Never." Max glanced down at Fran and called, "Which prize would you like, Doctor? The stuffed bear or the nickel-plated compact?"

She smiled up at him. "Whatever's biggest, of course."

Laughter ran out amongst the crowd.

"Of course." The even, white smile Max gave her made her knees go soft.

The crowd grew in numbers, their shouts of encouragement almost deafening. Slowly and methodically, Max raised the mallet one last time. The sun descended behind him, capturing him in its faint reddish glow. The crowd fell silent. A growl escaped Max's throat as he swung down the mallet. Up, up the meter went until...*ding.*

The crowd went nuts. With great show, Max pointed to an enormous stuffed bear hanging on one side of the booth. Thoroughly bested, Ranen shook his head sadly, then ambled over to the prize rack and took down the bear.

"Here you are," Max said, dropping the bear into Fran's waiting arms before dropping down beside her.

The weight of the stuffed animal nearly upended her, but she held her ground. "Are you sure this is the biggest one they have?" she asked, desperately trying to see her handsome companion over the bear's furry head.

Pressing the fur down to visibility level, Max found her gaze. Humor glowed in his eyes. And once she started laughing, he followed.

As the crowd dispersed, Ranen sat down on the edge of the platform and sighed. "How the devil are you going to get that thing on the plane, lass?"

Both she and Max instantly sobered. She looked

at him, and he at her. He smiled. She returned it—a silent agreement not to think or talk about what would happen after their two weeks were up.

"Have a good night, Ranen." After giving the man a clipped nod, Max snaked an arm around Fran's waist and whispered, "Let's go."

"Back to the palace?"

He shook his head. "I think we could use a few of those rides now."

"I think you're right." Melting impossibly closer into his side, she remarked dryly, "And the scarier the better."

Never in a million years would Fran have guessed that such a small, provincial fair would have something like...

"What is this ride called again?"

Max gave her a wink. "Legends of love."

Tucked away at the far end of the fairgrounds, where the ocean water could be filtered in, was one of the most magical rides. As the sun sank behind the horizon, disappearing for another day, lovely boats attached to an underground cable moved through four feet of water with the grace of a dolphin. Fran and Max had a boat to themselves with the bear perched up front as lookout. Grassy hills with fuchsia flowers gave way to covered bridges as she and Max enjoyed the ride, sitting arm in arm, hip to hip.

"From the stomach-dropping antics of the Octopus to the smooth sailing of Legends of Love." Fran gave him a nudge with her elbow. "That's quite a leap."

"Who says this ride is going to be smooth sailing, Doctor?"

"Are you planning on rocking the boat?"

That heart-stopping grin tugged at his mouth. "Thinking about it."

This time Fran's stomach dropped for an entirely different reason. A husky promise, a fierce gaze.

As twilight set in, the boat moved through the water as though its occupants hadn't a care in the world. And in the distance, it seemed that the switch that turned the din of the fair-goers to mute was flipped on.

"I've been on something similar to this back home," Fran informed him.

"Have you?"

"Yep." She turned, gave him an innocent look. "Tunnel of Love, I think it was called."

A muscle jumped in Max's jaw. "And with who did you take this journey?"

"Whom," she corrected with a smile. "With whom did I take—"

"Francesca…"

"Bert Wilson took me on that ride."

"And Bert Wilson was…?"

"My boyfriend."

"Ah." If his jaw got any tighter it might just break.

Her smile broadened. "He was my boyfriend in sixth grade."

Max's mouth twitched with amusement, his jaw relaxed. "Did he kiss you?"

"He tried."

"You didn't let him?"

"No way."

"Are you going to let me?"

Even in the coming darkness, his eyes looked incredibly blue, incredibly vibrant. She wanted to get lost in them. In him. Forever—or for as long as he'd let her. "Yes, Highness. You may have...one kiss."

"Just one?" Max draped an arm around her and pulled her closer.

She grinned at him. "I'll let you know."

Around them, the air grew cool. The breeze picked up. But Fran barely noticed the change. The other boats were far away, but Max's mouth was so near. The heat from his body seared her, and her anticipation grew. She moistened her lips, ready, so ready to feel his mouth on hers again. On a soft sigh, she let her eyes drift close—

Suddenly the boat jerked to a stop. Like a bucket of trout, she and Max pitched forward. With a gasp, Fran landed on the bottom of the boat, Max beside her.

"Are you all right?" Max took her face in his hands, his eyes searching hers.

"Yes." They were under a small, covered bridge. Rolls of misty white floated underneath, primed to consume them. Fran stared up at Max. "What's going on?"

"It must be six o'clock." He was so near, only a breath away.

"The fog?"

"Yes."

Despite the cool mist, Fran's blood began to heat. "Why did they stop the ride?"

His gaze fell to her mouth. "It's a safety precaution."

"I don't feel very safe, Highness."

"That's not what I want you to feel."

The fog took up permanent residence around them, creating a perfect little world where no one could get in and no one could get out. Exactly like the two ancient lovers had planned.

Gently, Max brushed a finger across her upper lip. Tiny shudders cascaded through her. She had to ask. Every part of her ached for him. "What do you want me to feel, Max? Tell me."

His blue eyes turned black. "Why don't I show you?"

Without waiting for a response, Max had her on her back on the bottom of the boat, his lips on hers. His kiss was fierce, filled with a need her body recognized and welcomed. And as his tongue plundered, she succumbed, groaning and whimpering, taking everything, giving everything.

But kisses weren't enough. Why weren't they enough? she wondered.

On a growl, he dragged his mouth from hers. For a moment his gaze swept her face. "You make me weak, Francesca." His eyes still pinned to hers, he moved his hand slowly under her blouse.

Her heart slammed against her ribs as Max cupped her breast through the thin cotton of her bra, gently kneading her swollen flesh. Fran swallowed a gasp, the pleasure so raw it almost frightened her. Was a simple touch supposed to feel this good?

"You are so beautiful," he whispered, his thumb flicking lightly across her tender nipple. "But it's much more than that. You're clever and funny and incredibly passionate." His gaze searched hers almost desperately. "I've never known anyone like you."

"Or I you," she said breathlessly.

A need, powerful and raw, raged through Fran's blood, then pooled low. She didn't understand this kind of desire—stretched to the point of breaking. Dennis had kissed her a few times, but that was all, no fireworks. She'd never had fireworks.

She'd only been with a man once. Mr. Smooth Talker. It was fast and uneventful. No soft touches, no ardent words, no tumbling heat in her womb. After that experience, she'd always regarded physical intimacy as something she could take or leave.

With a click, Max unclasped her bra. A draft of cool air touched her nipples, quickly followed by the weight of his warm palms. Two large hands raking up her bare skin, kneading her breasts, sending her mind and body reeling.

But control had no place here.

Giving in to the brazen woman that was desperate to be released, Fran put her hands over his and pressed his palms harder against her breasts.

Max cursed huskily, no doubt filled with the same need springing to life inside her. He dragged up her blouse, then lowered his head.

Fran cried out like a hungry child as his mouth made contact with her skin. She wanted to feel exposed, embarrassed by the act. But she didn't. She only felt desired as Max brushed soft, moist kisses down the slope of her breast.

But when his lips closed around her nipple, suckling deeply, she forgot all. Her mind went blank; her body hummed as he played her. It was a song she didn't recognize, but one she wanted to hear over and over.

"Tell me what you want, Francesca." His warm breath mingled with the stroke of his tongue as he urged her taut peak into pebble hardness.

"More." She hardly knew if she'd uttered the word aloud. All she knew was that she needed him, needed everything he could give her.

Abruptly, Max disappeared, down into the mist, uttering "Much, much more." That raspy promise sent splinters of heat and thrill to a place she barely recognized, a place that almost frightened her in its intensity.

The boat stirred on the water as the fabric of her skirt crept higher. Chilly air fluttered against her thighs, followed by powerful hands, thick black hair and a five-o'clock shadow. Soft, wet kisses moved up her inner thighs, higher, higher. His hands followed, massaging their way, until she could feel his breath against the wet heat of her own body.

Her mind whirred. Panic, only slight, but there. "Max, I've never—"

His lips brushed lightly across her panties, his warm breath shooting straight into her.

"Oh, please, I—"

"Francesca, trust me." Down came her panties. Up came his hands, his mouth.

She thought she'd go mad. With his finger poised at the entrance to her body, she truly thought she'd go mad.

Breath held, Fran waited, desperate for him to lead her out of this sweet misery. Slowly, inch by inch, he pressed upward, deep inside of her. Eyes falling closed, Fran sucked in a breath, her muscles clamping around him. Exquisite pleasure gripped her as she rode him slowly at first, then faster. And for one brief second, she thought nothing could ever feel so good.

She was wrong.

The moment his tongue made contact with her slick core, she died and was instantly reborn. No man had ever touched her, kissed her this way, and she was so thankful that it was Max. The man she loved. He sent her to a place where control no longer mattered. A place where she allowed herself to give in, give up.

With both hands and mouth, he sent her higher. He had her twisted and turning, whimpering his name, forgetting her own as she thrust her hips upward, trying to get impossibly closer.

And with the protective fog still surrounding them, Fran cried out, waves of red-hot electricity pummeling her core as she gave her body and soul to the man who demanded them both.

Eight

Maxim struggled for air as the throbbing below his waist nearly had him howling. He needed her, wanted her. Wanted to take her right there in the boat. His ears ringing with her soft cries, he knew that she wanted him, too, that her body was hot and ready, primed for more of what he'd just given her.

But he had no protection, no—

Suddenly the boat jarred, made the decision for him. The motor turned over and sputtered. The mist began to dissipate. Too soon, too bloody soon. He didn't have time for any more thoughts or queries. Before the mist left him and Francesca totally exposed, they had to get themselves back in order.

"What's going on, Max?" Her tone was weak, but it was filled with the same raw need that coursed through him.

"The ride. It's on again. The mist has quit early tonight. God knows why." Frustration gripped him. "Or maybe the devil."

A soft, very feminine curse pinged in the night air, accompanied by the shifting sounds of clothes being tugged and righted. "Does this happen very often...the, ah, fog ending early, I mean?"

"A few times a year." He knifed a hand through his rumpled hair. "Give me your hand." Maxim eased her up and onto the bench.

She turned to him, her eyes glowing, her cheeks pink. "Do you think anyone will know?"

"No." More than anything, he wanted to kiss her again. He wanted to forget where they were and how she'd made him feel. He wanted to do anything but think.

But instead, he reached out, smoothed down her hair, tucked a stray wisp behind her ear.

As the boat lurched forward, moved through the water toward the dock, their gazes remained locked. The wonder in her tawny eyes pulled at Maxim's gut. She wanted to know how he felt about what had just happened, wanted to know what he was thinking.

But she wasn't about to ask.

Just as he wasn't about to tell.

He turned away from her. Around them the fog packed up and left. But its departure didn't take the heat with it, the heat he could still feel from Francesca's body, or the taste of her on his mouth, or the music of her cry when she found release.

No, those things would be burned into his memory for years to come. What had happened here? He'd taken and given from many women in his time, and not once had he felt...stunned.

Being with Francesca had been different. And different was trouble.

Like a game that would never be won, he felt compelled to play. Why hadn't he left her alone the minute he'd met her? Why hadn't he stayed in Paris? Why had he offered up two more weeks?

Salty wind blew across his tight jaw. He'd pursued, he'd come home and he'd offered up because never in his life had he wanted anyone the way he wanted her. She got to him on all levels, and it made him nuts. And he knew that if he gave in, took what she was willing to give, he'd be faced with an out-of-control fire that he wasn't able to extinguish.

The boat docked and was tied up by the same lethargic-looking teenage boy that had sent them out more than a half hour ago. Maxim jumped onto the deck first, then helped Francesca out. She smiled shyly at him, uncertainty replacing the heat in her eyes. Maxim wanted to ram his fist into one of the pilings. He wanted to give her a solid answer. He wanted to give her what they both craved.

But this insane need to be more than just physically close to her made him want to run in the other direction.

She slipped a hand through his arm as they walked from the dock and into the chaos of the fair. "Tonight? How about a game of chess?"

The word *yes* fought for control of the word *no*. But an even stronger control, the one that kept him sane and productive and blissfully impassive, took over. "I have to work."

She didn't say anything for a minute, then, "All right. What about tomorrow?"

"Perhaps. I have an enormous project to finish."

"Someone once said, 'All work and no play…'"

"Yes. Perhaps balance is the key."

"And that's what you think you're doing, Max?" A sudden sharpness entered her tone, frustration. "A balancing act?"

Well, it was some kind of act, that was certain. If his need for her wasn't so great, his need for work would not exist. He changed the subject. "We left the bear in the boat."

Pausing at the entrance to the fair, she turned, looked up at him. Challenge sparked her eyes. "Maybe we should leave everything in the boat."

And like a true fool, he didn't rise to the occasion. "Maybe."

A dank chill hung on that word, hung between them. He watched her eyes fill with pain and confusion, watched as she dropped his arm and headed for the car.

Leave everything in the boat. What a bloody lie. How in the world could he ever think that today was the end, that he could just forget, move past, ignore? He couldn't.

She was under his skin now, in his blood.

"You are my sweetest boy."

Lucky yawned, then stretched out his chunky pup paws on Fran's lap. Dawn had arrived an hour ago

and Llandaron was just coming to life. Flowers
turned their heads toward the sun, anxious for sus-
tenance. Horses shifted in their stalls, waiting for
their oats.

Auspiciously, Lucky and his brothers and sisters
hadn't had to wait for the sun to rise. Glinda gave
them what they needed, whenever they needed it.

Blood pounded in Fran's temples, trailing slowly
downward into her cheeks. Last night, in a fog-
covered boat, Max had given her what she'd needed,
what she'd never experienced before. He'd made her
feel feminine and wanted. He'd made her think that
he cared for her.

But when the fog had lifted, he'd turned away,
took her home, said good-night. He'd done all this
with an air of cold indifference. Perhaps the keeper
of the fog had been kind to take away the misty
shelter before anything more had happened.

Obviously, around Max, she had no sense. Just the
fact that she had thrown caution to the wind, blindly
believing that he might actually care about her.
Hadn't she already experienced that kind of brush-
off from a man in the past? Why hadn't she learned
and avoided?

Fran stroked Lucky's coat as he nodded off. She
hadn't avoided it, because somewhere in the deepest
caverns of her heart, she believed that Max wasn't
like the smooth talker, that his brush-off wasn't about
male conquests.

Maybe she was just in love and stupid and hopeful.
But maybe not. Because of her past, she'd gone
through most of her twenties with her jerk-meter

turned on too high. No bad guys could get in. No good guys, either. Was she really about to give up, turn tail and run before confronting Max about what had happened last night?

"Hello, there."

Fran's head shot up. Blinding white sunlight pierced her eyes. She blinked repeatedly, barely able to make out the silhouette of the person who'd delivered that cheery, high-pitched, feminine greeting.

Holding up a hand to shield the sun, Fran squinted. "I'm sorry. I can't see you."

The figure moved closer, allowing the sun's brilliant glow to wash over and away. A slender woman, probably in her late sixties, stood a few feet from Fran in a long dress of white and silver. She was reminiscent of Audrey Hepburn, with what appeared to be white ballet slippers on her feet and a sapphire-and-diamond tiara sitting atop her short gray hair. There was no doubt that she was a member of the royal family. But if that was the case, why hadn't Fran seen her before?

"Good morning." The woman smiled. A very toothy, childlike grin that caused Fran to smile in return.

"Good morning."

"Dr. Charming, isn't it?"

The soft accent in her stately tone spoke of higher education and more than likely, the finest of finishing schools. But oddly enough, the regal woman didn't carry that I'm-so-much-better-than-you attitude that some Los Angeles yuppies did.

"Please, call me Fran." She made a move to

stand, but the older woman motioned for her to stay where she was. And with what could only be described as true poise, walked over and looked down into the whelping box.

"Glinda's done awfully well for herself, hasn't she."

Fran nodded. "Very well. They're all beautiful." And so was this woman, Fran mused. The closer she came, the more beautiful she looked. Fine lines etched her aristocratic features, soft pink tinted her high cheekbones.

"The king has promised me the pick of the litter." Interest lit the woman's wide-set violet eyes as she spotted the sleepy bundle in Fran's lap. "Who's this?"

"I call him Lucky."

Those incredible eyes turned on her. "He's the one you saved?"

"Yes."

"Very brave, Fran."

Fran shook her head. "Not at all. It's my job to—"

"To save others?"

"Sometimes."

"There is another who needs to be saved, Fran."

Fran's gaze flickered toward the whelping box.

A merry little laugh escaped the older woman. "No. Not in there."

"I'm sorry," Fran began, feeling totally confused, but intrigued. "I don't understand what you mean."

"You will, my dear." With a quick smile, she turned and walked back toward the patch of sunlight.

The silver dress and diamond tiara reflected the light, sending a hailstorm of sunlight back at Fran.

"Excuse me—" Fran paused, for she hadn't gotten the woman's name "—Your Highness? Wait, please."

But there was no answer.

And a moment later, the sun shifted in the sky and the woman was gone.

Work.

Maxim stared at the numbers on the page, trying to focus. But just as they had for the past six hours, the numbers fuzzed, turned to lines, then to snakes.

With great frustration, he shoved the papers off his desk. He'd been distracted more than a hundred times in his life and had still managed to get his work done. That is, until Dr. Charming had come to Llandaron. She was a thorn in his side, and he didn't know whether to curse her or venture out into the black night, go to her room and kiss her.

His gaze flickered toward the chess table. The table he'd stared at from the time he'd gotten home last night until close to three in the morning. What an idiot. Women did not become an obsession. They were an amusement. A good time had by all, so to speak. Both parties enjoying each other, then departing happy, content and, most importantly, alone.

The scent of the roast-beef dinner he'd yet to touch drifted through the air, mingling with the spiciness of the fire and something else…something, no someone…

Soft footfalls, clean, floral scent.

He cursed.

"Are you going to tell me what's wrong, Max?"

He released a weighty breath, but didn't look up. "How did you get in here?" He tried for a cold tone, but even a deaf man could hear the heat, the thrill, that broke through.

"The guards know me." She walked over, stood beside him.

His eyes remained on his desk. If he looked up into those eyes and saw need, want, he'd be dead in the water—or he'd be alive, with her, in his bed.

"And the door was unlocked," she continued. "Maybe it was unlocked for a reason?"

Ignoring the hopeful, almost apprehensive, thread in her voice, he said, "I'm expecting a package."

She placed a hand over his. "Well, here I am."

A grin touched his mouth. Sexy, spunky, irresistible woman. She made him crazy. He shook his head, but didn't remove his hand from under hers. "I thought we weren't going to see each other tonight."

"Because you had to work."

"Exactly."

"I don't buy it."

"Pardon me?" Without thought, he glanced up at her. His chest tightened, and the rest of him threatened to follow suit. It wasn't that she had on a see-through nightgown or a raincoat with nothing underneath.

She didn't need any of that. Dressed in just a simple blue sweater and jeans, her hair swept off her face in a loose bun, she looked heart-stoppingly beautiful.

Those tawny eyes blazed down at him. "Look, Max, if you've changed your mind about this, about us, I'm not going to stay here—"

"Nothing's changed."

"Then what's going on?"

His control was cracking like an oyster shell in a hurricane—that was what was going on. And if she didn't get out of here, he was going to strip her naked and taste every inch of her.

Control be damned.

No doubt taking his silence as a rejection, Fran let go of his hand and crossed to the fire. Her back to him, she asked, "Remember the day we met? Remember how we talked about choices?"

"I remember."

"Well, Max, right now you need to make a choice. You need to be honest."

The room pulsed with tension. Maxim stood, shoved his chair back. "You want honest? Fine." He crossed the room in four strides, grasped her by the shoulders and whirled her to face him. "I need you so badly my teeth ache. I've never needed anything, Francesca. Do you understand me? Never." He kissed her hard on the mouth. "But I need you."

Fran felt as though her heart might bruise her ribs it pounded so hard. She'd heard him correctly. Max wanted her, needed her. That encounter in the boat wasn't a mere passing fancy, just as his reaction afterward wasn't a rejection.

He was afraid to need, just as she was afraid to hope.

Looking up into his eyes, eyes that blazed with tenderness and passion, Fran knew that she could give herself to this man and walk away when the time came. She had grown since her encounter with the smooth talker. A real woman resided within her now. Ready to accept two weeks with the man she loved.

She'd given up control. Now she had to give up wishes and dreams for a magnificent reality.

With all the heat and force and love she felt, she snaked a hand to the back of his neck and pulled his mouth down to hers. Her lips rolled over his, plying him with short, soft kisses, tracing her tongue across his lips until he opened. Until he groaned into her mouth. And when he did, liquid fire erupted between her thighs.

His kiss was punishing and she took it, whispering a desperate ''Take what you need, Max,'' against his mouth.

He pulled away, though his mouth remained within inches. ''My future is not my own, Francesca. In a week and a half, during the masquerade ball, I must tell my country—''

''No.''

''Yes, dammit. You need to understand.''

''I do understand.'' She looked into his eyes, burning with desire. ''I'm no fool, Max. In a week and half I'll be saying my goodbyes. To Llandaron. And everyone in it.''

''You don't understand—''

"Yes, I do." Her words were forceful. Behind her, the heat of the fire assaulted her. Beads of sweat trickled down her back. "We have ten days left. Do you want to spend them apart, working...wanting each other?" She pressed against him, felt the evidence of his desire on her belly. "Or do you want to spend them together, in your bed?"

She watched as his eyes changed from black to electric blue. She heard the growl that escaped his lips and the glorious sound of defeat that followed.

"Damn this. Damn you."

His mouth was on hers in seconds, his arms around her, pulling her hard against his chest. A delightful shiver shot up her spine, making her breasts tingle and ache. Frantic, they groped at each other as Max took her tongue into his mouth, sucking, warring, playing, his heart slamming against her chest, causing her nipples to bead.

Her body was his, her heart and soul, too—if he wanted them. Feeling off balance, she clung to him as they made demands with their mouths. She tilted her head, desperate for his kiss to be deeper, desperate for something she'd only discovered a few days ago.

Longing to see him, feel his warm skin under her palms, made her restless. With shaky fingers, she fumbled with his belt buckle. Down went the zipper, off went the jeans. Not to be outdone, Max had her sweater over her head and jeans pooled at her feet in five seconds flat. The sounds of their breathing, heavy and husky, filled the room.

"Francesca, this won't be slow and sweet." He

gripped her backside, pulling her forward against him.

She gasped, totally vulnerable, totally lost. Frustrated with too many buttons, she tore the fabric of his shirt wide open. "I don't want slow."

"What do you want?"

"Just you, inside me."

With his gaze boring into her, he let his free hand trail down her belly until his fingers found the valley between her curls. "Here?" he asked, thrusting a finger inside her.

"Yes," she whimpered.

He slid another finger inside her. "More?"

"Yes."

Her body expanded, her mind melted as he thrust yet another finger inside her.

"Francesca," he uttered, hoarse, almost desperate.

"You. I want you. Please, Max."

On a rush of breath, he scooped her up and carried her into his bedroom. Gently, he placed her on the bed. Cool sheets kissed her heated skin. The mattress dipped with his weight. He reached for his side table, took out a foil packet and quickly unwrapped it.

"Let me." Fran smiled at him, took the condom out of his hand.

Her gaze found him, hard and thick and pulsing. She'd never looked this closely at a man, never wanted to. But with Max, she wanted everything.

Down his shaft she went, feeling every inch of him as he groaned, growing impossibly harder in her hand.

He became animalistic, pressing her back on the

bed, spreading her legs with his knee, burying himself inside her.

A gasp rushed from Fran's lips, and her nails dug into his back. His thrusts were deep and fast, and she met every one. Lifting her hips, grinding them against him, listening to the slap of their bodies as the moisture from their desire converged.

Breathless, she fought to hold on, but he pushed her over the edge. Her muscles contracted, her mind shot to the heavens, and her cry erupted into the air—air scented with lovemaking.

Driving into her like a madman, Max shuddered, his head dropping back. His fingers dug into her hips as release took him too.

After a moment, he rolled to the side, gathered her in his arms and held her tightly. A light sheen of sweat decorated his chest, his heart thrummed against her cheek. Fran smiled softly. She'd made love to the man of her dreams. A fantasy come to life. A grown woman's fairy tale.

She shut her eyes, trying not to think, not to remember the realities of their situation. She wanted this time to last. She wanted to tell him how much he meant to her. But as her body cooled and her breathing returned to normal, she knew she had to be brave.

"Maybe I should go back to my room."

Pulling her impossibly closer, Max whispered against her ear, "You're not going anywhere."

Brave *and* strong. "Sneaking in late or in the morning—someone will see." With a little maneuvering, she broke free of his possessive grasp, sat up.

"What happened to spending time together in my bed?" She could hear the pout in his voice.

Sheet wrapped around her, she stood. Lord, she could spend a lifetime in his bed, but it wasn't practical to think that way. She had to get used to leaving him if she ever wanted to survive losing him.

"Spending time in your bed was for…making love," she reminded him.

"Love 'em and leave 'em, huh?"

She laughed at yet another of his American sayings. "Get that one in Texas?"

"Kentucky."

"Ah."

Lightning fast, he reached out, snatched the bedsheet and tugged lightly. "Come back to bed, Francesca."

His eyes were liquid, highly seductive. He lay there, naked, fully erect again—all granite muscle and devilish smiles. Heat began to build between her legs.

To resist him was like resisting water in the desert. Impossible.

"Come back to bed," he repeated, tugging her closer, until she was inches away.

"To sleep?" she asked, her strength depleted.

"Yes." Eyes blazing, he rid her of the sheet. And with strong hands, he lifted her up, placed her atop his erection. "But later. Much, much later."

Nine

Fran couldn't stop grinning as she walked up the palace steps. Today, she believed in animals that sang show tunes, poison apples sent by wicked queens, and handsome princes who fought dragons by day, then made love to their lady by night.

A soft breeze blew her rumpled hair about her shoulders, and the early-morning sun felt warm on her skin. Or perhaps the warmth was the result of the wonderful night she'd spent with Max.

Her grin widened.

In all her adult life, she'd never imagined feeling so wanted, so needed…so filled with love. "Walking on a cloud" had just been one of those silly romantic expressions up till now, while the phrase "blissfully happy" had been an unattainable fantasy.

Nodding a good morning to the butler, she entered

the massive front hall. Sneaking out of Max's bed, scooting back to the castle and up to her room before most of the staff was awake had sounded like a good idea. She didn't want gossip.

But like any lady in love, she couldn't help wishing she'd stayed, naked and warm beside her prince. Besides, who was going to see her at this time of morning except the butler and maybe a maid or two?

"Good morning, Doctor."

Fran dragged in a breath, anxiety knotting within her. Spoken too soon. Slowly, she turned, eyed the king, who was decked out in an ensemble that fell somewhere between casual and couture. "Good morning, Your Highness."

"Fine day."

"Yes." Why did she have to sound like a frightened little mouse?

"You're up early."

Her hand immediately flew to her hair. How much of a wreck did she look? "Yes, I was just…"

"Checking on Glinda and the pups?"

"Yes." The lie rolled off her tongue far too easily. Why was she even pretending? More than likely, the king knew exactly where she'd been.

Her brow furrowed. He knew where she'd come from, and yet his inquiry had been extremely tactful. A gentleman. He hadn't wanted to embarrass her.

The king rubbed a hand over his bearded jaw. "Charlie tells me you've taken quite a shine to one of the pups."

"I adore them all, Your Highness. But I must confess, I do have a special bond with number six."

"Perhaps when you return to America, you might wish to take him along."

Fran's mouth fell open. Was he serious? Take Lucky home? "Really?"

With a bright smile, he nodded.

"He's still too young yet, but—"

Waving a hand, the king amended, "When he's of proper age, he will be brought to you."

Fran stared, speechless. The king was incredibly generous, as well as a true gentleman.

"Consider it my gift to you," he continued. "For all your hard work and dedication."

"Your Highness, being here for Glinda and the pups is my job. Honestly, you don't have to give me anything."

"I want to, Francesca."

A wave of apprehension swept through her. Had the king ever called her by her first name before? She didn't think so.

Something was off here, but she couldn't quite put her finger on it.

"Llandaron is a wonderful place." This time, the smile he bestowed on her didn't make it to his eyes—serious eyes. "But its charm can be deceiving."

That wave of apprehension surged upward into a forty-foot curl. Deep in her gut, where feminine intuition dwelled, she knew that the offer to take Lucky home wasn't a generous gesture of thanks for a job well-done.

The true reason came out a few moments later...

"We do not live a fairy-tale life here." The king's lips thinned. Then he took a deep breath and continued. "No. No fairy tales. Not for the royal family, at any rate. We do not have the luxury of reverie. Our life, our commitment to our people, are of utmost importance. We must give them stability and leadership. Our responsibilities to them are very, very real."

Like Alice in her wonderland, Fran seemed to shrink under the man's gaze. Not because his warning was offered with a malicious undercurrent. Quite the opposite, actually. The expression in his eyes was one of dismay, worry. And it made her feel sorry for him.

He didn't like what he'd said, yet no doubt he felt he'd had to say it.

Where once there had been euphoria in Fran's heart, melancholy now reigned. How could she look this man in the eye and tell him she understood? That come the end of next week, she was leaving with no illusions about his son?

Probably because she wouldn't believe the claim herself. To be honest, she did have illusions. She couldn't help herself. Especially this morning. Foolish woman, she hoped to God that Max would fall in love with her.

The King's brow creased with concern. Perhaps he only needed her to nod her understanding. But she couldn't even do that much. She just wanted to escape. Her room seemed a hundred miles away, by dogsled, in frigid temp—

"Oliver? Where did you run off to?"

Fran released the breath she didn't know she'd been holding and glanced over her shoulder. A woman in a pale yellow dress appeared in the doorway of the morning room. It was the woman who'd come to the stables yesterday.

"I'm coming, Fara." The king gave Fran a gentle smile. "If you will excuse me, Doctor, my sister insists on breakfast at this hour. She's been in India for two months and has just returned. Her internal clock is a bit off."

Fran inclined her head. "Of course."

She watched the king walk away, wondering why she wasn't hotfooting it up the stairs, taking advantage of a quick getaway. Maybe because she was waiting for some sign of recognition from the beautiful princess. As if on cue, the woman called Fara smiled at Fran, gave her a wink, then disappeared into the morning room after her brother.

Mystery solved, Fran mused as she trudged up the steps. The king's sister. Max's aunt.

Another member of this royal clan who no doubt cared for their country and its people above all else. Such a commitment should be admired and totally understood. So what was her problem? She'd been a good girl, a responsible woman, her whole life. For goodness' sake, she was set to open a high-tech surgery facility, her dream come true. She should understand duty and honor. She should be able to accept the fate and, more importantly, the choices of others.

It was just that the choice of never seeing the man she loved again caused her heart to squeeze in anguish.

Fran and her hangdog countenance trudged into

her room and plunked down on the perfectly made bed. The king's words, his warning, rolled over her like a bucket of icy water. Llandaron was a country in need of leadership and stability. Max was not their fairy-tale icon, no matter how much he looked like one. No, he was a man of the people. Or as he had put it last night, a man whose future was not his own.

Fran stretched out on top of the mattress. Over the next nine days she would keep reminding herself of that. If not just to understand the realities of the situation, but to be able to leave this country with a little dignity and her heart intact.

Max glanced up. "You ate all the potato chips, Doctor."

She raised a brow. "That's because you took a half hour on that last move."

He chuckled as his gaze moved over her, the glow of the full moon outside illuminating half her face, while the fire lit the other. She was so beautiful. The way each smile she gave him meant something different. The way she wrinkled her nose when she was concentrating on her next move. She looked as good sitting here by his fireplace as she had in his bed.

The lower half of him contracted. Why did he crave her every moment? In bed and out?

Before she'd come here, he'd rarely dated a woman for longer than a week. He'd just lose interest. One woman would have an incredible figure, the other, an incredible mind. Never the twain would meet.

But Francesca had everything. Brains, beauty, humor, passion, drive, compassion, understanding. They had been together for almost a week now, going to town, to the beach, to bed, and Maxim felt as though he was just beginning to know her.

"Be forewarned," she said, resting her chin on her palm and smiling broadly. "If you continue to spend over five minutes on a move, I'm going to devour those cheese curls *and* your chocolate milk shake."

"Threats are going to get you nowhere."

"Nowhere?" She raised a brow suggestively.

An amused growl escaped his throat. "Brat."

She dissolved into laughter. "Sticks and stones, Highness."

"Break bones?"

"You know that saying?" She captured his pawn with one of her own. "What a shocker."

His gaze dropped from her eyes to her lips to her breasts. "Don't make me toss aside these pieces and take you right here on the chess table."

The fire crackled and spit as Francesca reached across the table, placed a finger under his chin and lifted. "Come on. No empty threats to distract me or get me to forfeit the game."

"Forfeit?"

"Don't think I don't see what you're up to. I'm winning here."

"You're daft. Look at my position." Capturing her finger, he removed it from under his chin and gave the tip a soft kiss.

With mock effrontery, she snatched her hand back. "Trust me, Highness, I *have* been looking at your position. That's why I'm so confident."

He grinned at her. "Perhaps you would like another wager?"

"Fine."

"Any suggestions as to what—"

"Clothing."

He raised a brow. "Clothing?"

She nodded, her eyes as bright as the flames that licked the smoldering logs in his fireplace. "After each capture, the opponent must remove one piece of clothing. I imagine that the quicker you get to checkmate the least amount of clothes you'll lose."

"Or the slower you go…"

"Yes." Though self-assurance was written in her posture, the two pink spots that dotted her cheeks told an entirely different story.

"Ready, Highness?"

"I've never been more ready, Doctor." He sent his bishop two spaces, capturing a pawn.

Those pink spots deepened, but cool as dawn she removed an earring. Then after a deep breath, she took her queen out and captured his bishop.

A slow smile broke on his face. As she watched, he whipped off his shirt in one fluid motion. When his gaze found hers again, she was staring at his chest, her tongue darting out to lick her dry lips. He fairly groaned. If they finished this game, it would be a miracle.

Maxim forced his gaze back to the board, his mind only half working. He moved his pawn and took one of hers. With shaky hands, she slipped off another earring.

Maxim grunted. "So you're going to play like that, are you?"

"Like what?" she asked innocently.

"Jewelry does not count as clothing."

"No?"

"No."

"All right, Mr. Rules and Regulations." She reached under the table, and when she lifted her hands, two sneakers dangled from her fingers.

"Not much better," he muttered. "But at least you're not cheating."

She tossed the shoes onto the rug and stared at the board. Two minutes later, she'd moved in position to take his knight with her queen.

Chuckling, he captured her queen. "A little distracted, Doctor?"

Her gaze darted around the board. She was no doubt wondering why she hadn't seen such an enormous move, and more importantly, why she hadn't stopped it.

"Francesca, you will be naked and beat by the time that clock chimes ten."

She glanced up, fire in her eyes. "Don't count on it, Highness."

Ten minutes later, which happened to be nine-forty-five, Max sat there in nothing but his jeans—socks, shoes and belt, gone. His gaze roamed over his heavenly opponent. Shirt, bra and panties were all that remained. And of course, that honey scent that was signature Francesca.

Determined to see her beat, and to see her, period, Max took out his queen and captured her knight.

With a grimace, Fran reached under her shirt, unhooked her bra, then eased it out through an armhole.

"Clever, Doctor."

She immediately took his rook with hers and retorted, "Thank you, Highness."

"Looks as though we are both distracted." Maxim stood, unzipped his fly and stripped off his jeans. When he glanced up, Fran's gaze was traveling over him.

He tilted a brow. "See something you like?"

"A great many things." Her mouth twitched with amusement. "But I won't be fully satisfied until you're naked."

"Right back at you." He chuckled, sat down. His eyes scanned the board. Which move, which piece. Fighting for a moment of clarity, he willed himself to think past each move until suddenly he saw it—the end of the game. If he wanted to, he could put her in checkmate right now. But this was a game he wanted to win slowly. Watching her remove that shirt and strip of lace at her hips was far more interesting than an easy victory.

He took one of her remaining pawns with one of his, then sat back.

Her brow knit as she looked up at him. "You missed a great move."

"My mind wanders." Reaching back, he laced his hands behind his head. "To the beauty of what I am about to witness."

"About to, huh?" With a smug smile, she stood and slipped off her panties. The shirt she wore was long enough to cover her most intimate areas.

And before he could even groan with frustration, she moved her rook to within two spaces of his king. "Check."

Maxim suppressed a chuckle. She was rattled. Not thinking. His bishop was waiting, hanging out in the corner of the board hoping for the chance she'd just offered him.

And as he eased his bishop across the board, slowly, oh, so slowly, she sucked in a breath.

"No way!"

"Yes, Doctor. I want to see that beautiful chest of yours and I will."

Her gaze flickered toward the bishop, then chin lifted, she stood. With unsteady fingers, she opened one button of her shirt at a time. In the firelight, he could see her nipples, pebble-hard through the fabric.

Chest tight, he watched as she moved up, up, a thin strip of smooth belly and creamy torso assaulting his vision. Pausing, she looked at him, her fingers poised on either side of her unfastened blouse.

Her gaze dropped to his lap, where he was rock-hard and ready. "See something you like?"

"You're such a tease." He heard the husky tone in his voice and hoped she couldn't hear the flicker of desperation that accompanied it.

Slow and easy, she opened her blouse. Her beautiful breasts stood high and proud, nipples tight and rosy. Maxim gripped the arms of his chair as he watched her ease the fabric over her shoulders, then let it fall.

His jaw followed suit.

Without care or thought, he rose to his feet, stood in front of her. "Close your eyes, Francesca."

Apprehension glowed in her tawny eyes, but she did as he asked. Leaning close, he kissed her eyelids, her cheeks, then her mouth. She opened for him, but he wasn't ready to take. Not yet.

"Listen closely, Francesca."

"All right."

His hand darted out toward the chessboard, his index finger toppling his king. "Did you hear that?"

She nodded.

"I give up."

Her eyes snapped opened. She looked at the board. With a swish of her hand, she, too, toppled her king. "We both lose." Her eyes returned to his as her hands went to his waist, and pulled down his boxers. "And we both win."

Skin met skin, hard met soft, and Maxim lost his mind.

He had her back on the carpet in seconds. Poised above her, he stared into her eyes and knew he'd never see freedom in his country or in his heart.

An invisible fist slammed into his gut. He forced all thoughts aside, leaving space only for pleasure. Beneath him, she moved, arched, told him exactly what she wanted. Her skin glowed pink with desire. Her breasts rose and fell as her breathing grew heavy. Her hand snaked around his neck, pulled his face down to hers.

Her hot, wet mouth met his in one long, luscious kiss. He wanted to forget everything but her. And she made fulfilling his need possible, opening her legs wide. Moving down, he nuzzled her breast, then took her nipple between his lips, his teeth.

Her cry turned his manhood to stone. No one had ever responded to him the way she did. So unguarded, her soul open, her body willing.

"Make love to me, Max. Now. Please."

Her whimper made his blood heat. Made him grind his hips into her. He felt her warmth, her slick dampness.

He cupped her face, rubbed his thumb across her lips, red from his kiss. "Let me get—"

"No." Reaching behind her, she burrowed into the back pocket of her jeans, came out with a condom. She smiled up at him, breathless. "I'll take care of it."

"Where did you get that?" Was that jealousy he was feeling? Jealousy that ran like hot candle wax through his veins as he wondered why she had condoms.

"From my overnight case. A girlfriend helped me pack. She must've stuck condoms in there as a joke." She grinned, lifting her hips. "But I'm sure glad she did."

He released a breath, a moan, as relief filled him. "Why are you glad, Doctor? Are you hoping to get lucky?"

Her hands snaked around his waist, gripped his buttocks. "Do I need to hope, Max?"

In response, he snatched the foil packet from her hand, ripped it open and quickly sheathed himself. "No, Francesca. All you need to do is wrap your legs around me and hold on."

She grinned like a tigress as she wrapped her legs around his waist. With one breath, Maxim rose and then thrust deep inside her.

He wasted no time. His hands filled with her breasts, he drove into the wet heat of her body with hard, deep strokes. Over and over again.

She wanted more, needed more—he could see it, feel how she gripped him. He slipped his hand between them, his fingers between her curls. And as he thrust into her, he stroked her core.

Higher and higher they went. Fast strokes, gulps of air. Until Francesca called out, called his name and stiffened. Tight, hot fists surrounded Maxim. He reared back, slamming into her as he took his release.

After a moment he collapsed to the side, taking her with him. He listened as her breathing slowed and evened, listened as she fell asleep wrapped in his arms beside the dying fire.

What had started out as a simple affair and a way to rid himself of a freedomless future had turned into something more—something he'd never felt in his life or wanted to feel, for that matter: true affection.

Would five days be enough time?

He pulled her closer. It had to be enough.

Time flew by just like the birds overhead. Her feet in the water, her backside on the dock, Fran gazed up at the flock of gulls that sailed across the blue sky. A perfect day to sit beside the ocean and fish— and steal kisses from the man she loved.

She turned to Max, who was reeling back to cast

his line for the tenth time in five minutes. "Has it been eight hours or eight days?"

"I'm not counting and neither should you." His line shot forward, the clip just missing her arm.

"Mind your hook, Highness."

"Terribly sorry." He rewarded her with a grin. "Milady."

In rolled-up jeans and a T-shirt, shoot, he looked good. He had a boyish quality today. Not a care, not a prince. She could almost forget who they were and where they were.

Almost.

She raised her line out of the water to see if her worm was still there. It was. "One time, when my father took me fishing, I got a little crazy with the whole casting thing myself."

He tried to look shocked. "Not you."

"Hard to believe, I know."

A dry chuckle left those perfect lips. "What did you do? How crazy are we talking here?"

"Hooked my father's ear."

"You didn't."

"Yes, unfortunately I did." She reached over and touched the soft lobe of his right ear. "I had no idea that the ear could bleed that much."

"I'm intrigued. You don't speak of your family very often."

No, she didn't. And she preferred it that way. But since she'd opened this can of worms… "I don't really have a family anymore." She stared out at the ocean. "My mother died when I was a baby. And

then when my father died, I was left with my stepmother and two stepbrothers. We never got along.''

''Why is that, do you think?''

She sighed. ''To paint you a picture—they wear
fur, I save fur.'' With a shrug, she added, ''They're
not horrible people, just different, not family. You're
so lucky to have a family who cares about you,
Max.''

He didn't agree, but offered something more personal. ''My mother also died when I was young. Of
pneumonia.''

''I'm sorry.''

''I am, as well.'' He didn't elaborate; perhaps he
couldn't. ''She had a very different outlook on life,
on Llandaron. Like you, she believed in choice.''

''She sounds wonderful.''

He turned to look at her. ''Francesca, were you
hoping that Dennis was going to be family?''

She nodded.

''I'm sorry if I was the cause of—''

''You weren't. Dennis is a friend, not a husband.''
Out at sea, a fishing boat drifted. ''I rushed things.
Next time, I'll need to take it slower.''

''Next time?'' The question sounded light enough,
but she could swear she heard an underlying trace of
irritation.

''Next time.'' Heat surged into her cheeks as she
continued to ride this out-of-control train. ''You
know, with a boyfriend. I'll take my time to see if
he's…husband material.'' Her stomach rolled. She
didn't want anyone else. She wanted Max as her boyfriend, her husband.

"I don't like this conversation," he grumbled.

"Neither do I."

The crash of ocean waves and the caw of gulls ruled the silence for a good two minutes. Then Max tossed his pole on the deck and grabbed her hand. "Let's go for a swim."

"I don't have a suit."

He raised a brow.

"Oh." Her gaze fell, her cheeks burned. "But the water is still pretty cold."

"I'll keep you warm."

Anticipation fluttered in her belly. "Okay."

Easing her to her feet, Max gave Fran a soft kiss, then led her off the dock and onto the strip of secluded beach. Every step they took toward the water's edge, a piece of clothing was shed.

In the water, Max gathered her in his arms, held her close. Fran closed her eyes, wrapped her legs around his waist and tried to forget that in three days she would be on a plane to California.

Ten

The cool grass felt wonderful under Fran's legs. Today was going to be a hot one. As spring inched toward summer, a ninety-degree day would shoot up during a stream of mild seventies. But Fran didn't mind. Like clockwork, the ocean sent a cool breeze every few minutes, as though commanded to do so by royal decree.

Beside her, under a large white birch, the puppies played in a pen that Charlie had set up for them. They were growing like weeds, had healthy appetites and lively dispositions.

Especially her Lucky. He was a little clown. Smiling down at him, Fran wondered if the king would actually follow through on his promise to send the puppy to her when he was old enough.

Oh, she hoped so. The thought of leaving here with nothing but memories made her heart break.

As one of those decreed breezes whipped up around her, Fran turned her attention to Ranen Turk and the lovely Princess Fara. Under the guise of seeing to the pups and making sure he understood all of Fran's instructions regarding care for them after she left, Ranen had come to the stables. But as soon as he'd seen Fara out on the lawn playing croquet, he'd headed there.

It didn't take a psychic to see that Ranen had a serious crush on the woman. He was actually smiling. Fran smiled, too, as she observed the pair. While one was dressed in an expensive pale-lilac morning gown, the other was garbed in grass-stained pants and a homespun shirt.

Well, opposites did attract, didn't they? Fran mused. Look at her and the prince.

Max.

His name reverberated through her blood. She really missed him. Called away on an urgent business matter, he'd left for London this morning and wouldn't be back until tonight. Anger and frustration bit at her. They didn't have much time left. Tomorrow was the masquerade ball. The next day, she was leaving.

Despair assailed her. But she pushed it away. After all, didn't she need to get used to missing him?

"Her Highness bested me once again."

Fran's gaze jerked up to see Ranen and Fara walking toward her.

"Don't let him fool you, Fran." Amusement flickered in Fara's voice and in her violet eyes. "He graciously allowed me to win."

The old man plunked down beside Fran. "I'm not gracious."

Fara laughed. "Of course you are."

"Women." He rolled his eyes, but Fran couldn't help noticing how his chest puffed out and his cheeks took on a rosy hue.

"I suggest you both call it a draw. That's what Max and I—"

Fran froze, her mouth agape. Rewinding her mental recording device, she listened to what she'd just said. Max and I? *Max and I!* How red was her face? What was she thinking, saying something like that?

Granted, most people knew that she and the prince hung out together, as friends, maybe more. But to use such a familiar, personal phrase… She might as well have a sign around her neck that read I Love Prince Maxim.

Fara smiled down at her. "You were saying, my dear?"

Fran returned the gracious and tactful woman's smile. "Just that it's better for both parties to win, that's all."

"The girl is right, Ranen."

"The girl is a romantic."

"What in the world is wrong with that?" Smoothing her skirt, Fara added, "If I recall correctly, you were very fond of romance at one time."

"That was a long time ago," Ranen grumbled good-naturedly.

"Is that so? Well, then, I suppose I shouldn't ask you to escort me to the ball tomorrow night."

Ranen's eyes went wide. "Ah, tosh. You know I'd be honored to take you, Fara."

As though she'd expected Ranen to come to heel all along, the princess smiled brightly, nodded at him, then turned to Fran. "Speaking of the ball, what are you planning to wear, my dear?"

Wear? Fran hadn't thought of that. The ball marked her last night with Max. Of course, she wanted to look her best when he saw her—when he held her close, danced with her until the sun came up. "I have a black cocktail dress."

"No, no, my dear." Reaching out, the older woman patted her shoulder. "That won't do at all."

"But I don't have anything—"

"I do." Brilliant stars shone in her eyes. "Shall we go to my rooms, try a few things on?"

Fran couldn't stop the wave of anticipation that took hold of her. To wear a royal gown, yards of silk or satin, lace... Her pulse jumped. "I would love to go with you, but the puppies really shouldn't be left—"

"I shall watch the pups, lass," Ranen declared, giving both women a grin. "After all, I will be their keeper when you depart for America."

"Thank you, Ranen," Fran said, coming to her feet.

Fara smiled at Ranen. "Come for me at seven-thirty?"

"I will indeed, Highness."

As Fran and Fara walked away and up the palace

steps, the princess chatted excitedly. "I have the perfect dress in mind, my dear. White, strapless, fitted waist and meters of skirt. It will look beautiful on you, with your hair up, your eyes shining. And I shall lend you one of my tiaras, too."

"Oh, I couldn't do that."

"You could and you will."

The palace door was held open by the stoic but ever-present butler. Fara breezed through into the entryway and up the steps. "On the night I wore this dress, the fog rolled in as thick as a velvet curtain and stayed well past seven. You see, when the fog dissipates early or late, magic is afoot."

Fran had flashes in her memory of a boat with an ardent pair of lovers. Yes, magic...

"I remember my maid remarking that something big was about to happen. And she was right." At the top of the staircase, the princess paused, grinned at Fran. "My father was having a soiree that night. When I walked into the dining room, I immediately noticed a dark-haired man with darker eyes. A Frenchman. A barrister. I was instantly attracted to him."

"Sounds intriguing." And familiar, Fran thought as they walked down the hallway.

"All through the night, we remained together. Talking, dining, dancing. He looked at me in a way no man had ever looked at me. I fancied myself in love with him. And when he left, I could think of nothing else."

"What happened?"

"He sent me many letters asking me to come to him."

"And did you?" Why did her chest feel so tight, her lips so dry?

"No, I did not."

"Why not?"

"I think you know why, my dear. 'Tis not my problem alone." The princess paused at the door of her suite and turned to look at Fran. "But although I stayed true to my country, to my station in life, I never married. Could not."

Fran swallowed hard. Why was the woman telling her this? What was the moral of her story? To convince Max to abandon his sense of duty? Or go home with understanding and acceptance?

"So what happened, Highness?" Fran heard the desperation in her voice, but could not quell the sound. "Did you ever see him again?"

"Only in my dreams." Fara placed a warm hand over Fran's cool one. "Perhaps Maxim has more courage than his aunt." On a weighty sigh, she turned, reached for the knob and opened the door to her bedroom. "For all of our sakes, I truly hope so."

The fog was slowly disappearing as Maxim stepped up to the lighthouse door. Once inside, wondrous scents greeted his nostrils. Scents he hadn't encountered since childhood. He noticed Francesca's purse on the hook where she always kept it. Peace moved through him.

"What the devil goes on in my house?" he bellowed with good humor.

"In here, Highness."

Ah, that voice, husky and honeyed.

For close to fifteen years, he'd walked into this house and heard nothing but ocean waves. Back then, he'd liked the solitude. But somehow, when the addictive Francesca Charming had charged into his life, she'd upset the delicate balance of everything; she'd changed him. She'd made him need her.

And most significantly, she made coming home to a freedomless existence bearable.

Dropping his bags in the hall, he darted up the stairs, stood in the doorway of the kitchen. His gaze moved over her.

Hair pulled back off her face, Francesca stood in front of the stove, attending to a large piece of meat. She wore a simple cotton sundress in several shades of blue, and her feet were bare. His chest tightened at the domestic sight. She looked as though she belonged.

She also looked over at him and smiled.

"Good evening, milady." His greeting came out like a growl. But his response couldn't be helped. Especially when she smiled at him like that, her cheeks flushed from the heat of the stovetop.

"Have a good day?" she asked as he walked over to her, gave her a peck on the cheek, then stood behind her.

"Not bad." Wrapping his arms around her waist, he whispered in her ear, "Better now."

She smelled good, felt good. Why couldn't he have this every night? Just them, sharing dinner, sharing their lives—

Maxim stopped himself right there. Thoughts like that had no place in his mind. "You didn't have to make all of this, Francesca. I could have—"

"I wanted to." She pressed her back against his chest. "By the way, your guard let me in. Obviously some tenacious and very spoiled royal dude had a talk with him about letting one Dr. Charming come and go as she pleases."

"Wonder who that was."

"Yeah, that's a toughie." She laughed and turned back to the stove.

Resting his chin on her shoulder, he asked, "What are you making?"

"Your favorites." With a long silver instrument, she pointed to the smoking meat. "Whiskey-baked ham and potatoes."

Memories flooded his senses. Long ago, when his mother had been alive, she'd insisted that the palace cook make whiskey-baked ham and potatoes for him every Sunday night. His heart contracted. No one had ever found out such a thing; no one had ever cared that much.

"Thank you." He kissed her softly on the neck, held her close. "How did you know…"

"Your aunt told me."

"You spoke with Fara?"

"She's very informative. We had a long talk about you as a boy."

He chuckled. "Bloody hell."

Glancing over her shoulder, she lifted an amused brow. "Why would you tie your sister to a tree, then leave her?"

"We were playing. Cathy was a Brit. I was a Scot. I only left her for an hour or so to get us both some lemonade."

"Likely story." With her own chuckle, she turned back to the stove. "And what happened? You were waylaid or something?"

"Yes. Exactly." Did Francesca know that her simple sundress hugged every curve? If someone was to walk in right now and see them, what would they think? Happy couple?

Need raged inside him. He needed to be close to her, needed her to rid his mind of all thought, all want, and just feel.

"What or *who* waylaid you?" she asked, pressing back against his chest, her bottom against his groin.

Perhaps she needed to be close, as well, he mused.

"A certain chambermaid's daughter." Reaching down underneath that simple sundress, Maxim found Francesca's bare and incredibly smooth legs.

She released a soft moan. Up, up his palms moved, feeling every inch of her thighs. He wanted to make her happy, make her forget, make her lose herself in him for as long as possible.

Dropping her kitchen gear, she let her head fall back against his shoulder. "Women are your distraction, Highness." She was breathless as his hand moved across her belly, down to the lacy strip at her waist.

"Only one woman," he growled, slipping his fingers inside her panties, gently cupping her woman's mound. And he meant it, in every sense. He could not do without her.

She dragged in a gasp. "Here? In the kitchen?"

"Right here."

"What about the food?"

"Later." As he'd hoped, thought deserted him as the moisture from her body, from his touch, met his fingers.

The princess and her lady's maid clasped their hands together and sighed. "Maxim, along with a hundred other men, will not be able to tear his eyes from you tonight, Fran."

In the full-length mirror, a woman Fran had never seen before stared back at her. Her shimmering blond hair was piled on top of her head, wisps of curl weaving through the diamond tiara Fara had lent her. Her makeup was flawless and her eyes held a brilliance only excitement could give—excitement and hope.

Her neck was slim and long, her bare shoulders, soft and elegant. White elbow-length gloves dressed her hands and wrists, while the gown of her dreams clung to the curves of her body, all white satin and tulle. And at the bottom of the skirt as well as at the bustline, a seamstress of incredible skill had embroidered a beautiful pattern of black.

If she didn't know any better, Fran would have sworn that the woman she saw in the mirror was a princess.

But she wasn't.

Not that that bit of truth was going to stop her tonight. For better or worse, she was Cinderella, off to the ball. Fran lifted the skirt and smiled at her white satin pumps. Off to the ball in her not-so-glass slippers.

"Are you ready, my dear?" Fara glanced past her in the mirror and righted her own diamond tiara, which was studded with sapphires.

Fran smiled at the beautiful older woman in her elegant blue silk gown. "More than ready, Highness."

"You look perfect."

"Thank you. And I don't just mean for the dress." Fran turned, faced the woman. "I mean for everything."

The princess touched her cheek and said, "My pleasure, my dear," then took her hand and led her out into the hallway. But instead of taking the normal route down to the main part of the house, Fara guided Fran through several passageways she'd never seen before. Secret passageways.

Minutes later, they emerged to the sound of jubilant voices, polite laughter and orchestra music.

"Here we are," Fara said as they came to the landing of a grand staircase—a staircase that led straight into the ballroom.

Apprehension grew within Fran, mixing with anticipation to form a heady brew. Below them, the party was in full swing. The staff flew about the glorious, gold-encrusted ballroom, serving champagne and caviar. Women in gorgeous gowns danced and mingled with men in tuxedos.

Fran glanced up. The ceiling had been painted to resemble a sky at twilight, complete with stars and crescent moon. The walls held massive family portraits. She recognized Max immediately, and her heart fluttered like a schoolgirl's.

The scene was totally surreal for an unsophisticated vet from L.A. But she was keen on surreal. Tonight, she embraced surreal.

Laughter bubbled up from her throat as she followed Fara down the stairs where Ranen waited, decked out in a dark-brown suit and a wide grin.

But over in the opposite corner of the ballroom, Prince Maxim Stephan Henry Thorne awaited the arrival of Francesca. He watched her walk down the steps with the grace of a gazelle, took in her tentative smile and was filled with a need he knew would never be quenched.

Beside him, two women were trying to coerce him back into their conversation. But he paid them no attention. His gaze remained on the most beautiful woman in the world. She reminded him of the swan that skimmed the surface of the pond near the stables. Elegant, striking and just a tad bit aloof.

Excusing himself, Maxim made his way over to her. But he was too late. By the time he reached the stairs, she'd been scooped up by the Marquis de Petrenburg and whisked onto the dance floor.

Maxim gritted his teeth. So that was how it was going to be? He should have expected such a response. She was a newcomer, vivacious and incredibly beautiful. The men of the court were going to trip over themselves to get an introduction. Obviously he would have to show them to whom Francesca belonged.

As soon as the music ended, several of the men

took off like thoroughbreds at the starting gate, on their way to ask her to dance. But Maxim got there first.

"May I have this dance, Doctor?"

She whirled around. Her tawny eyes glowed with happiness when she saw him. "You look very handsome tonight, Max."

"And you look stunning."

She smiled. "Thank you."

He took her into his arms as the music began, light and fanciful. "I didn't think I would get a dance, prince or no."

"What do you mean?"

"You're a hit with this lot."

She leaned forward and whispered, "But am I a hit with you?"

His chest tightened as he moved across the floor. She made him crazy—with want and wonder and too many things he didn't want to name.

If he kissed her right here, in front of the many prominent members of the Llandaron, British and Scottish court, what would happen? And did he give a damn?

He pulled her closer, his gaze drilling into hers. They danced two more numbers this way, totally absorbed in each other.

"I know there are many other women who are waiting to dance with you, Highness." She tilted her chin. "Maybe we should give them a chance."

"No." He didn't give a whit about any other woman. "Only you tonight, Francesca. Only you."

Before she could respond, the music ended and a

footman tapped Maxim on the shoulder. "The king wishes to see you, Your Highness. At once. In the library."

Where moments ago passion had existed, anger now resided. Maxim knew exactly what his father wanted with him. The old man had warned him about what would befall him tonight.

Maxim squeezed Fran's gloved hands. "I'll be back."

"Hurry up." She gave him a wink. "We only have until midnight."

"What?" His gut tightened with alarm.

"I'm kidding. Cinderella, the prince, midnight..."

He nodded soberly. "Right."

Five seconds after he'd walked away, Charles Crawford, the trust-fund playboy with half a brain and a splendid ego, descended upon Francesca. Hands balled into fists, Maxim stalked out of the ballroom and into the library.

The king sat in his favorite chair, a brandy in his hand. "I have spoken with the duke of Ernhart. He has offered his daughter in marriage."

Maxim remained standing. "Has he? How generous of him."

"Sarcasm has no place in matters of the state."

Or in matters of the heart.

"Maxim, I have given you every chance to find yourself an acceptable bride." The man shook his head. "You leave me no choice."

"We all have a choice, Father." Francesca's words.

Maxim went to the sideboard and poured himself a brandy.

"Llandaron needs its royalty," the king continued. "There is no disputing that."

"No, there is not."

"You are their hope now, Maxim."

"My brother—"

"Your brother has not produced an heir. God knows if he ever will. We cannot wait."

Maxim drained his glass. What was he fighting here? His father's control or his own? His want versus his duty to his country? Reality was cruel, but there was no escaping it. His choice was duty, had to be. He raked a hand through his hair. If only Francesca was—

No. Hell, no. Even if she could, he cared far too much about her to offer her this life. To someone who has lived their life in freedom, bondage would be unbearable.

But he wanted her. Wanted no one but her.

"I will announce your betrothal at midnight."

Maxim gave his father a hard stare. "Why wait? If I'm going to give my life to my country, you might as well take me now."

He had to get to Francesca first. He had to hold her in his arms and explain what she'd never allowed him to explain.

But Francesca didn't need an explanation.

Huddled against the library door, Francesca's limbs, heart and soul went numb as every scrap of hope she'd clung to over the past several days died.

Max was to be married. Not to her, but to a woman he didn't even know.

Tears burned tragic pathways down her cheeks. He'd made his choice. He'd chosen his country.

Backing away from the door, she stumbled down the hallway. The beautiful dress that had made her feel like a princess just thirty minutes ago choked her now, reminded her that fairy tales are just stories for children with innocent hearts.

Tears trembling in her eyes, she moved quickly, up the stairs and to her room. She'd be damned if she'd stick around to hear Max's betrothal announced. Her time in Llandaron was over. After a quick goodbye to Glinda and the pups, she was leaving.

Once in her room, she stripped off the gown and placed it on the bed. She would write a note thanking Fara for her generosity—leaving out the woman's heartfelt wish that Max's courage would supersede her cowardice.

Brushing away the salty wetness from her face, Fran knew that she would also leave out the fact that she, too, would never love another, never marry and never forget the one man who had made her believe that true love existed.

Eleven

"**S**he's gone." Breathless with rage, Maxim stalked the library floor. To his right, the clock struck 3 a.m. What had he done? What had he allowed to happen here?

To his left, his father sat on the couch, calm as bathwater, his wrinkled hand wrapped around an empty brandy snifter. "I don't understand your distress, Maxim. You have walked away from many women."

Maxim gave the man a hostile glare. "I didn't walk away this time."

"What I mean to say is that you have parted company with many women."

"Francesca is different."

"Is she?"

"Yes, damn you!" Halting at the fireplace, Maxim rapped his fist on the mantel.

Knuckles met sharp stone. But he barely felt the sting. Francesca had left without a goodbye. Without giving him a chance to explain, to hear his choice.

He drove his hands through his hair. His bloody choice. Why had she come here and told him that he had a choice at all? Why had she come here and made him want more than what he had been offered?

He glanced toward the ceiling and muttered, "How the hell did she get out of here and on a plane back to America so fast?"

"I helped her."

A sound, guttural and untamed, surged from Maxim's throat as his gaze shot to the doorway.

With a pipe nestled into the side of his mouth, Ranen Turk shrugged. "I had to help her, Highness."

Maxim's lips thinned in fury. "Why?"

"I care for her."

"So do I!"

Crossing the room, Ranen put a hand on Maxim's shoulder. "She didn't want to be here when your marriage was announced."

"My marriage..." Maxim's head reeled, and the walls closed in around him.

"Can you blame her, Highness?"

"I don't understand this." Maxim's eyes narrowed on his father. "Did you tell her?"

The king sat back in his chair. "No."

"Then how did she know you would announce my

marriage tonight? There is no way she could have—''

Maxim froze. Had she overheard him and his father talking, planning his future? Had she come to find him and heard his acquiescence?

A stream of curses fell from his lips. What a fool. What a bloody fool he was.

''I'm sorry about this, Maxim,'' the king offered on a weighty exhale.

Maxim's chuckled bitterly. ''Are you?''

''What are you saying?''

''Are you sorry, Father?''

''Highness—'' Ranen began, but was instantly cut off.

''Isn't this what you want, sire?'' The latent anger inside Maxim suddenly leaped to life. The anger that had resided in him since he'd found out that his brother couldn't produce children. The anger that soared up to claim him every time he thought about living a life with restrictions, limitations and few personal choices. ''Isn't this a perfect solution? The commoner gone so your son will fall in line?''

The anger that gripped his heart at his own inability to stand up to his father.

Crimson tides moved through the king's cheeks and jaw as he bellowed, ''Maxim Thorne, you are a grown man. Yet you speak like a child.''

Maxim stood there, blank, amazed, feeling as though he'd just had his ears boxed. Falling into the chair beside his father, he scrubbed a hand over his face. How had he allowed himself to fall so far? He'd been acting like a child ever since he'd learned his fate. Why was he so surprised that the king had treated him like one?

Respect wasn't given, it was earned. And if he wanted to claim respect, he needed to act like a man—not a prince, but a man. And decide his own future and his own fate.

Maxim sat back in his chair, spoke calmly. "I will not marry that woman."

"Why?" the king asked quietly.

"Because I do not love her."

"Is there another that you love?"

Maxim opened his mouth, ready to explain to his father that what he felt for Francesca was nothing as simple as love. Need, want, possessiveness, maybe. Not love.

But that would be a lie.

Maxim drained his glass. The heat from the brandy didn't dull his senses as he'd hoped. Instead, the amber liquid infused his heart, bringing the truth to the surface. With Francesca, nothing was simple. With her, life was wonderfully complex and intense. Just as their love would be.

Yes, he loved her. With every breath, every cell of his being.

"Yes, Father. There is another that I love." The words felt good and strong and right on his lips.

The king's blue eyes flickered with strife. "Why didn't you tell me this, son?"

"You knew I was seeing her. That she stayed—"

"Seeing is not loving. Love is an entirely different matter."

"Even to you?"

"Yes."

"You understand that my country, my people, they mean everything to me." Maxim's tone was serious, self-assured.

"But?"

"But I will marry whom I choose." His jaw set firmly, Maxim stared intently at his father. "Whom I love."

The king said nothing, merely nodded.

"And as we all, in our own particular way, helped the woman I love to leave—" Maxim's gaze flickered toward Ranen, then back to his father "—we all will help to bring her back."

"What do you suggest?" the king asked.

Ranen puffed thoughtfully on his pipe. "Mary Trost has a pregnant sow due any day now. Fran would be most helpful—"

"Sit down, Ranen," Maxim commanded on a dry chuckle. "Let us put our heads together."

The king raised his brow at Maxim. "This is your choice, my son?"

"*She* is my choice, Father."

The old man nodded. "Your mother wanted love for you, Maxim. As I didn't see you looking for such a requirement, I..." The king paused to clear his throat, then said softly, "The queen would have been proud of you."

An invisible fist tightened around Maxim's heart as he nodded. "You, as well."

The lines dusting the corners of the king's eyes crinkled with laughter. "I think you're right."

Ranen groaned, rolled his eyes toward the ceiling.

"Enough of this horse plop. We've a plan to configure. I really would like some help with that sow."

Father and son grinned.

"She went back to Los Angeles, to her clinic." Maxim didn't add, *back to Dagwood*.

She wouldn't fly back into that dull vet's arms the minute she returned home, would she? A bolt of jealousy shot through him. No man but him would touch her. And after he sank to one knee, after he apologized for his insanity, after he kissed the breath from her lungs, she would tell him that she forgave him, that she loved him, too.

"I think I may have the perfect solution." The king's exclamation ripped Maxim from his thoughts. "But you won't be able to leave for another week, Maxim."

"I can't wait a week, Father."

"Trust me, Maxim." The king smiled. "Trust me, son."

Spring had eased into early summer. Los Angeles buzzed with new heat, new films, new loves and new families—especially canine and feline families. Owners brought in new litters for their first checkups and first rounds of shots.

In the past, seeing all the young animals had been a joy for Fran. But not so much anymore. Sure, they were cute, but they were also a constant reminder of Glinda, the pups and her little Lucky.

And the prince.

Her heart dipped. God help her, she missed him and Llandaron and everyone who lived there. Over the past week, she'd gone out with friends, seen a couple of movies, jogged by the ocean—anything to keep herself sane. But at night, in her bed, her thoughts went to him. Drifted over the ocean to him.

"So, Doctor, what's wrong with her?"

Fran's gaze snapped up. Standing across the metal examination table was Amanda Randall, a beautiful redhead who'd taken off her shirt in her last movie. That was the kind of clientele her clinic catered to. Last year, the idea had sounded wonderful, lucrative, a real path to her dream of opening the surgery facility. Now, it felt...silly.

But life tumbled on. Obviously her life was the clinic, Los Angeles, the plans for the new surgery facility. Maybe she needed to have some patience. She'd readjust.

"Miss Randall, Chardonnay has fleas."

The starlet's green eyes filled with horror. "Impossible."

To prove her diagnosis, Fran ran a thin-toothed comb through the Pomeranian's fur, then held the metal object up to the light. "Would you like to see—"

"No." The suggestion apparently insulted her.

Pampered celebrities, fun and wonderful? Where had Fran ever gotten that idea? "Have you been giving her the flea control product I gave you?"

"Well, *I* haven't." She snorted. "That's Jerry's job."

"Jerry?"

"My personal assistant."

"Of course."

The woman tucked a perfectly coiffed curl behind her ear and informed Fran, "I have to be on location in Miami next month. I want to take Chardonnay, but…well, eeuuwww."

To be fair, there happened to be a couple of pretty normal celebs who came into the office. But sadly, they were few and far between.

Or maybe it was just that nothing seemed real and normal anymore, nothing but Llandaron.

Lord, how was this possible? When she'd first stepped onto that small island nation, she'd swore she was in a fairy tale. Yet when she'd left, she'd felt as though she was leaving the only real life she'd ever known.

"So what should I do now?" The woman's query had many sides to it and many answers—for them both.

For Fran, the answer was this: do her work and try to forget. A week had passed since she'd left Llandaron. Max hadn't tried to contact her. Not that she'd expected him to. He was probably making plans for his wedding.

With a sharp inhalation, Fran snipped off the end of a tube of flea-control lotion and applied it to the dog. "This will take care of the rest of the month. But bottom line, if you don't want fleas in your house or on Chardonnay, you'll have to do it yourself."

"Or get a new assistant."

"That would work, too."

After a quick thank-you, the woman put on her gloves, held the dog at arm's length and carried her out of the office. Dennis passed the starlet in the doorway. He offered her an amiable smile, then turned to Fran.

"Busy day."

Fran nodded. "Very."

On returning home, she and Dennis had instantly reverted back to being friends. It was how they'd begun, and it was good.

His brow knit as he stared at her. "Are you all right, Frannie?"

"Fine." If living with a broken heart was fine.

"Listen," Dennis said, helping her pick up the paper towels, cotton balls and empty flea-control packet. "It's pretty close to quitting time—do you mind if I beg off early?"

"Got a hot date?" she joked.

"Yes, actually."

Fran stilled. "Oh."

"Does that bother you?"

"No, not at all. Actually, that's great. I'm really happy for you." And jealous, not because she felt anything more than friendship for him, but because he had a special someone and she'd lost a very special someone.

He smiled at her. "There's one last patient. An emergency."

"I'll take it. You go ahead. And have a great time."

"You have a great time, too, Frannie." He gave her a wink, then trotted out the door. A few seconds later she heard him say, "Right through there."

Fran laughed halfheartedly. Must be a pretty great date if he was acting so—

A soft gasp escaped her. Tears pricked her eyes. But she was too stunned to cry.

"Max?"

"Doctor."

That irresistible smile, those Prussian-blue eyes. His gaze pinned on her, he stood in the doorway, looking like a dream, a mirage, in perfectly tailored black pants, white shirt and black jacket.

"What are you doing here?" Her heart crashed against her ribs, over and over. Why was he here? For work, for her?

"We would have been here sooner, but someone needed their shots first." From behind his back, he pulled out a large puppy. "Someone needs you, Francesca."

"Lucky?" She crossed the room, took the sleepy puppy in her arms.

"Yes, I brought Lucky. But he's not the one who needs you."

Her knees turned to butter, her throat tightened as she looked into Max's eyes. "He's not?"

"No, he's not." Reaching out, Max cupped her cheek with his right hand. "When you left Llandaron, I went crazy. You've changed me, Francesca. From a prince to a man—flesh and blood and bone."

Fran melted into his palm, fear and hope mingling in her belly. "Tell me why you've come here before I go crazy, too."

"I can't live without you."

Fran fought to keep her balance. "And the horsey-looking Danish princess…"

"There is no princess." He leaned toward her,

kissed her softly on the mouth, whispered against her parted lips. ''There's never been anyone but you.''

Her pulse beat awkwardly, then flew to the heavens. It's what she'd wanted to hear, was desperate to hear. And yet… ''What about your country, the people…?''

He pulled back slightly so he could look deep into her eyes. ''They adore you, and they want my happiness.''

''And your father…''

''My father was only waiting to hear me say I loved you.''

Tears pricked her eyes, and she held Lucky closer to her chest—for support and for protection. ''You said that you loved me?'' The words sounded heavenly. But could she believe? Could she turn and embrace hope one last time?

And if so, was it possible to come out the victor?

''I love you, Francesca Charming.'' He said the words simply and with ultimate sincerity, then took her in his arms and held her and Lucky close. In her ear, he whispered huskily, ''Remember that first day we met and you talked about choices?''

She swallowed hard, said breathlessly, ''I remember.''

''My own bloody fear kept me from making the right choice. My fear of losing control kept me from seeing the truth.'' He pressed a kiss to the top of her head. ''You made me see the truth.''

''Oh, Max.'' The sweetness of his words nearly had her undone.

"You are a part of my soul, Francesca, as I am a part of yours."

"Are you sure you want this, Max? That you want me?" She needed him to be sure. For herself as much as for him—for the life and the future that lay ahead.

He tipped her chin up, gave her a long, teasing kiss before saying, "I've never been more sure about anything in my life."

It was all she needed to hear. "I love you so much, Max. More than I ever thought possible."

"Then come home with me, my beloved princess."

Her heart squeezed. Not from pain, but from happiness from a want and a need that had finally been offered. "To Llandaron?"

"Yes. You can still practice there. There are so many animals that need you, need your special brand of care."

Tears flowed down her cheeks, and in her arms her little Lucky yawned contentedly. A mere month ago she'd been a cynic. A woman who desperately wanted to believe in things her heart had warned her to discount. But now, here she was, beside the man she loved, her prince—and she knew that fairy tales sometimes did come true. And because she'd believed in true love, true love had believed in her.

Her eyes were filled with tears of joy and love when she looked up at Max. "I love you more than I can say. And I'll go anywhere you choose."

He kissed her again, and it felt as though they were back in his lighthouse, the sounds of ocean against rock surrounding them. "Marry me, Francesca," he whispered. "Be my wife. My princess."

"Yes. Oh, yes, Max."

"Let me give you children. Let me give you a family."

How well he knew her. A blissful warmth wrapped around her heart as she looked into the eyes of the man who would be her husband, her children's father and the prince of her heart forever. She had everything she had ever imagined, ever wished for in the deep recesses of her heart. A home, a family, a practice. And most importantly, Max.

She grinned up at him. "This really is a fairy tale."

"Yes, it is." The love in his words matched the love in his eyes. "And you know what they say at the end of a fairy tale?"

"You and your expressions." Her laughter bubbled in the air. "What do they say, Your Highness?"

Gently, he pulled her closer, kissed her deeply, then gave her a devastating grin. "And they lived incredibly, passionately, fortuitously and undeniably happily ever after."

* * * * *

And now,
Turn the page for a preview
of Laura Wright's
next sensual Fiery Tale,

SLEEPING WITH BEAUTY

Available in May 2003
from Silhouette Desire

One

Princess Catherine Olivia Ann Thorne sat pole-straight between her father and her aunt Fara at the head table, watching the people of Llandaron eat, drink, dance and be merry. Tonight, they celebrated the return of her brother Maxim and his wife, Fran, from their month-long honeymoon. They celebrated the couple's fantastic news of their pregnancy.

They celebrated love.

Almost unearthy music drifted up from the six-piece orchestra, encircling the brightly lit room. Scents of roast lamb and summer heather joined in the dreamy rotation, creating a blithe, warm atmosphere in the ballroom.

But inside Cathy, a cold heaviness dwelled.

Her gaze moved over her brother and new sister-in-law as they danced, so close, eyes locked, mouths turned up into intimate smiles.

Anyone could see how desperately in love they were. And it wasn't that Cathy begrudged them such happiness. Not in a million years. She loved her brother to death, and thought the world of Fran. She just wanted to feel a little of that happiness—a little of that love—for herself.

"Your tour of Eastern Europe has been extended another month, Catherine."

Cathy's stomach clenched at her father's words. She'd only returned from Australia three days ago, yet her social secretary had her scheduled to leave for Russia at the beginning of next week.

And now, another month was being tacked on.

"You look pale, Cathy dear," Fara remarked, her violet eyes narrowed with concern.

The king touched his daughter's gloved hand. "Are you feeling all right?"

"Yes, Father." No, Father. The mask of composed princess fought the restive, reckless woman that resided deep in Cathy's heart. Over the last several months something inside of her, in her mind and soul and blood, had started to wilt. Frustration built day by day, tour after tour.

She loved the visits and the work, but she was just plain old exhausted.

Cathy stood up, dropped her silk napkin beside her untouched plate. "I'm pretty tired. If you'll excuse me, Father, Fara."

She barely waited for them to nod. With a grace she was born and bred to, she walked out of the room, into the empty hall and up the stairs, her lavender ballgown swishing against her unsteady legs. Months of supervised, heavily guarded travels, dictated protocol and hounding press made her need for privacy akin to the need she had for air. The quiet, albeit temporary, sanctuary of her bedroom sounded like heaven.

But the way to her room was blocked.

"That mane of amber curls and those amethyst eyes."

Perched on the landing stood a portly woman, gnarled with age and garbed in a long tank dress of reds and purples, ropes of tangerine beads hanging from her neck. Cathy didn't recognize her.

"You are every bit as beautiful as I told your mother you'd be, lass."

Cathy gripped the banister, memories of the wonderful woman she'd barely known flooding her. "You knew my mother?"

"Aye. I knew the Queen." The woman's thin lips twisted into a cynical smile. "When you were just a speck in your mother's belly, I asked Her Royal Highness to allow me to read your future. But she refused my gift. Laughed at me, she did."

The woman's anger sat like a spoiled child between them, immobile unless appeased. A strange surge of unease coursed through Cathy. "Who are you?"

The old woman ignored the query. "I gave the King and Queen my gift regardless. Aye, I told them that you would be beautiful and kind and clever. I told them that you would be spirited and brave." Her large brown eyes darkened. "I told them that if they did not take great care of you…"

Cold fingers inched up Cathy's spine as the woman's voice trailed off. But she refused to show her fear. She forced on her finest royal countenance and said, "I think you need to finish the story."

The old woman's yellow smile widened. "I told your father and mother that if they did not take great care, they would lose you."

"Lose me?"

"Aye."

Deportment all but dropped away. "What are you talking about?"

"Cathy, you up there?"

The call shot between Cathy and the woman, breaking the trance that seemed to hold them both captive. Whirling around, her heart pounding in her chest, Cathy saw Fran coming up the steps.

"What's wrong, Cath?" Her sister-in-law's eyes were filled with apprehension.

"It's this old woman. She's—"

Fran cocked her head, glanced past her. "What woman?"

Cathy stilled, her pulse pounding a feverish rhythm in her blood. Slowly, she turned. The woman was gone.

On legs that had gone from unsteady to water-filled, she lumbered up the stairs, saying nothing, Fran following closely behind her. Cathy tried not to wonder where the old woman had disappeared to— or if there had been a woman at all. Was she going nuts?

As they entered the bedroom, Fran asked softly, "Are you all right, Cath?"

Cathy sat on her bed, shoulders falling forward. No, she wasn't all right. She was completely and totally overwhelmed. She turned to Fran and explained, "I'm a twenty-five-year-old woman who's rarely been alone, rarely known happiness and never known love. I'm so bloody tired of living on other people's terms, you know?" She searched her new sister's eyes. "Do you understand what that's like, Fran?"

Fran sat down beside her, took her hand. "Yes, actually I do. Until I met your brother, I hadn't lived at all."

"Why is that, do you think? Were you afraid to live or—?"

"I think I was afraid to believe that love existed for me." A soft smile graced Fran's mouth—the smile of a woman who now knew differently. "I'd been hurt pretty badly, and I didn't want to feel that kind of pain again. But your brother offered me a second chance."

Cathy sighed. "I'd like a first chance—to live. I deserve one."

"Of course you do."

Seven years of thoughts, plans, midnight fantasies and heartfelt hopes leapt through Cathy's brain. Was she brave enough? Weary enough? Desperate enough to grab hold, take what she wanted?

Perhaps the crazy old woman had come with a warning, not just a story from the past. A warning from her mother and maybe even from Cathy herself, that if she continued on this path, living in unhappiness—not really living at all—she'd truly be lost.

A shadow of fearfulness grazed her heart, but she brushed it away. "You're my sister now, Fran. Can I count on you?"

Fran squeezed her hand. "Just tell me what I can do."

"Help me pack."

*   *   *   *   *

Silhouette®

Desire®

Whom does Joanna Blake kiss on New Year's Eve?

Find out in:

RENEGADE MILLIONAIRE
(SD #1497)

by Kristi Gold

Available March 2003
at your favorite retail outlet.

**The passion
doesn't stop there.**

Don't miss Kristi's next
romance:

MAROONED WITH A MILLIONAIRE

Available June 2003

Silhouette®

Where love comes alive™

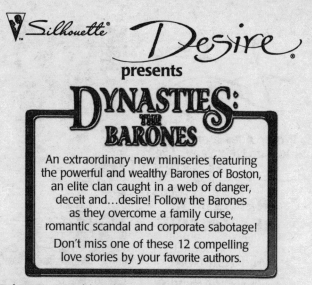

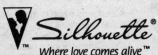

They weren't looking for each other…
but the chemistry was too powerful to resist.

MARY LYNN
BAXTER

A string of deadly warnings convinces Dallas mayor Jessica Kincaid to hire
bodyguard Brant Harding. But as their personal agendas intersect, Jessica and
Brant find themselves at odds, yet drawn to each other with a passion neither
can deny. And when the threat to Jessica's life intensifies, not even Brant's best
efforts may be enough to save her—or to buy them both a second chance.

HIS TOUCH

"Ms. Baxter's writing…strikes every chord within the female spirit."
—Sandra Brown

On sale February 2003
wherever paperbacks are sold!

MIRA®

eHARLEQUIN.com

For great romance books at great prices,
shop www.eHarlequin.com today!

GREAT BOOKS:
- **Extensive selection** of today's hottest
  books, including **current** releases,
  backlist titles and new **upcoming** books.
- **Favorite authors:** Nora Roberts,
  Debbie Macomber and more!

GREAT DEALS:
- **Save every day:** enjoy great savings
  and special online promotions.
- *Exclusive* online offers: FREE books,
  bargain outlet savings, special deals.

EASY SHOPPING:
- Easy, secure, **24-hour shopping** from the
  comfort of your own home.
- **Excerpts, reader recommendations**
  and our **Romance Legend** will help
  you choose!
- **Convenient shipping and
  payment methods.**

Shop online
at www.eHarlequin.com today!

INTBB2

Where Texas society reigns supreme—and appearances are *everything*!

Coming in March 2003
LONE WOLF
by Sheri WhiteFeather

The Native-American love child of a Mission Creek patriarch, Hawk Wainwright carried a big chip on his shoulder and made sure everyone in town knew he wanted nothing to do with his blue-blooded heritage. But Hawk found his heart softening for his beautiful but troubled next-door neighbor, Jenna Taylor. Could Hawk put his anger aside and come to the rescue of a woman who stirred his soul in every way?

Available at your favorite retail outlet.

Where love comes alive™

COMING NEXT MONTH

#1495 AMBER BY NIGHT—Sharon Sala
Amelia Beauchamp needed money, so she transformed herself from a plain-Jane librarian into a seductive siren named Amber and took a second job as a cocktail waitress. Then in walked irresistible Tyler Savage. The former Casanova wanted her as much as she wanted him, but Amelia was playing a dangerous game. Would Tyler still want her once he discovered her true identity?

#1496 SLEEPING WITH HER RIVAL—Sheri WhiteFeather
Dynasties: The Barones
After a sabotage incident left her family's company with a public-relations nightmare, Gina Barone was forced to work with hotshot PR consultant Flint Kingman. Flint decided a very public pretend affair was the perfect distraction. But the passion that exploded between Gina and heartbreakingly handsome Flint was all too real, and she found herself yearning to make their temporary arrangement last forever.

#1497 RENEGADE MILLIONAIRE—Kristi Gold
When sexy Dr. Rio Madrid learned lovely Joanna Blake was living in a slum, he did the gentlemanly thing and asked her to move in with him. But his feelings for her proved to be anything but gentlemanly—he wanted to kiss her senseless! However, Joanna wouldn't accept less than his whole heart, and he didn't know if he could give her that.

#1498 MAIL-ORDER PRINCE IN HER BED—Kathryn Jensen
Because of an office prank, shy Maria McPherson found herself being whisked away in a limousine by Antonio Boniface. But Antonio was not just any mail-order escort. He was a real prince—and when virginal Maria asked him to tutor her in the ways of love, Antonio eagerly agreed. But Maria yearned for a life with Antonio. Could she convince him to risk everything for love?

#1499 THE COWBOY CLAIMS HIS LADY—Meagan McKinney
Matched in Montana
Rancher Bruce Everett had sworn off women for good, so he was fit to be tied when stressed-out city girl Melynda Cray came to his ranch for a little rest and relaxation. Still, Melynda had a way about her that got under the stubborn cowboy's skin, and soon he was courting his lovely guest. But Melynda had been hurt before; could Bruce prove his love was rock solid?

#1500 TANGLED SHEETS, TANGLED LIES—Julie Hogan
Cole Travis vowed to find the son he hadn't known he had. His sleuthing led him to Jem—and Jem's adoptive mother, beguiling beauty Lauren Simpson. In order to find out for sure if the boy was his son, Cole posed as a handyman and offered his services to Lauren. But as Cole fell under Lauren's captivating spell...he just hoped their love would survive the truth.

SDCNM0203